W9-DHL-584

"Why didn't we stay together?"

She should have expected it. In a way, it was surprising that he hadn't asked before. "I don't see any need to go into it," she said, folding her arms. She saw no need to open old wounds—mostly hers.

His jaw set in a stubborn line. "It was because of my job, wasn't it?"

Abby drew in a breath, and let it out slowly. "Whatever happened back then, those days are over, Ryan."

"And what about the nights?" With that quiet question he stepped forward to close the gap between them. "Did I leave you alone then, too?"

He'd moved too close to let her feign indifference. Close enough to have certain memories flaring to life. Much too close for her comfort. She saw the challenge in his eyes. "Do you mean to tell me that if I kissed you right this minute, you wouldn't feel anything?"

"You're not kissing me," she informed him in no uncertain terms.

And then he was.

Dear Reader,

Welcome to Harlequin American Romance, where you're guaranteed heartwarming, emotional and deeply romantic stories set in the backyards, big cities and wide-open spaces of America. Kick starting the month is Cathy Gillen Thacker's *Her Bachelor Challenge*, which launches her brand-new family-connected miniseries THE DEVERAUX LEGACY. In this wonderful story, a night of passion between old acquaintances has a sought-after playboy businessman questioning his bachelor status.

Next, Mollie Molay premieres her new GROOMS IN UNIFORM miniseries. In *The Duchess & Her Bodyguard*, protecting a royal beauty was easy for a by-the-book bodyguard, but falling in love wasn't part of the plan! Don't miss *Husbands, Husbands...Everywhere!* by Sharon Swan, in which a lovely B & B owner's ex-husband shows up on her doorstep with amnesia, giving her the chance to rediscover the man he'd once been. This poignant reunion romance story is the latest installment in the WELCOME TO HARMONY miniseries. Laura Marie Altom makes her Harlequin American Romance debut with *Blind Luck Bride*, which pairs a jilted groom with a pregnant heroine in a marriage meant to satisfy the terms of a bet.

This month, and every month, come home to Harlequin American Romance—and enjoy!

Best,

Melissa Jeglinski
Associate Senior Editor
Harlequin American Romance

HUSBANDS, HUSBANDS... EVERYWHERE!

Sharon Swan

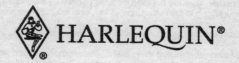

TORONTO • NEW YORK • LONDON
AMSTERDAM • PARIS • SYDNEY • HAMBURG
STOCKHOLM • ATHENS • TOKYO • MILAN • MADRID
PRAGUE • WARSAW • BUDAPEST • AUCKLAND

If you purchased this book without a cover you should be aware
that this book is stolen property. It was reported as "unsold and
destroyed" to the publisher, and neither the author nor the
publisher has received any payment for this "stripped book."

For all my great friends in Illinois

ISBN 0-373-16939-6

HUSBANDS, HUSBANDS...EVERYWHERE!

Copyright © 2002 by Sharon Swearengen.

All rights reserved. Except for use in any review, the reproduction or
utilization of this work in whole or in part in any form by any electronic,
mechanical or other means, now known or hereafter invented, including
xerography, photocopying and recording, or in any information storage
or retrieval system, is forbidden without the written permission of the
publisher, Harlequin Enterprises Limited, 225 Duncan Mill Road,
Don Mills, Ontario, Canada M3B 3K9.

All characters in this book have no existence outside the imagination of
the author and have no relation whatsoever to anyone bearing the same
name or names. They are not even distantly inspired by any individual
known or unknown to the author, and all incidents are pure invention.

This edition published by arrangement with Harlequin Books S.A.

® and TM are trademarks of the publisher. Trademarks indicated with
® are registered in the United States Patent and Trademark Office, the
Canadian Trade Marks Office and in other countries.

Visit us at www.eHarlequin.com

Printed in U.S.A.

ABOUT THE AUTHOR

Born and raised in Chicago, Sharon Swan once dreamed of dancing for a living. Instead, she surrendered to life's more practical aspects, settled for an office job, concentrated on typing and being a Chicago Bears fan. Sharon never seriously considered writing a career until she moved to the Phoenix area and met Pierce Brosnan at a local shopping mall. It was a chance meeting that changed her life, because she found herself thinking, what if? What if two fictional characters had met the same way? That formed the basis for her next novel, and she's now cheerfully addicted to writing contemporary romance and playing what if?

Books by Sharon Swan

HARLEQUIN AMERICAN ROMANCE

912—COWBOYS AND CRADLES
928—HOME-GROWN HUSBAND*
939—HUSBAND, HUSBANDS…EVERYWHERE!*

*Welcome to Harmony

Don't miss any of our special offers. Write to us at the following address for information on our newest releases.

Harlequin Reader Service
U.S.: 3010 Walden Ave., P.O. Box 1325, Buffalo, NY 14269
Canadian: P.O. Box 609, Fort Erie, Ont. L2A 5X3

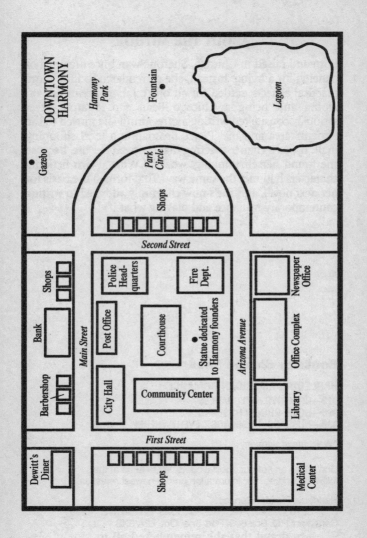

Chapter One

A man who once had sworn he would never forget her looked her straight in the eye with a blank expression, as if he'd never seen her before in his life.

Abby couldn't help but stare herself, thinking that unless Ryan Larabee had an identical twin with the same brilliantly blue gaze, it had to be him. And since she recalled quite well that his only sibling was an older sister, it was definitely Ryan.

She knew that. She was just having trouble convincing her vocal cords to say something to him, which was understandable. After all, it wasn't every day that a woman met a dangerously attractive male from her past, one she'd never expected to see again, even if she hadn't managed to block out all thoughts of him. To find that very male calmly standing on the doorstep, looking at her as though she were a complete stranger, was a startling experience, enough to leave anyone's throat frozen.

And Abby could only produce one hard swallow.

It was the tall and lanky man facing her who finally broke the silence. "Are you, ah, by any chance Aunt Abigail?" he asked in a deep voice tinged with a Western drawl that she remembered all too well. His halting tone seemed to indicate he'd been anticipating someone older.

"No, I'm not," she got out at last after another swallow.

He reached up and thumbed his black Stetson back from his forehead, revealing short, thick strands of dark brown hair. "I called earlier about a room. Someone said there were plenty available."

She cleared her still-tight throat. "That would have been one of my godmother's friends who helps out here. My godmother, who's out of town at the moment, owns this house and runs Aunt Abigail's Bed and Breakfast. As it happens," she added very deliberately, "I was named after her."

"I see," was his reply.

She didn't doubt he would have more to say shortly, when total recall hit, which was bound to occur after she told him what she was about to tell him. Her appearance had changed over the years, she had to concede. Certainly she was no longer a starry-eyed twenty-three. But despite the fact that she now wore her hair in a neat chin-length style rather than down past her shoulders, and favored tailored blouses and slacks over more casual tops and jeans, this had to jar his memory in a big way.

Bracing herself, she said, "I'm Abby Prentice."

All he did was continue to gaze down at her blandly. "I'm Ryan Larabee. If there does happen to be a room available, do you suppose I could come in?"

For a stark second she still couldn't move, and then she stepped back carefully, opening the front door wide. He entered, holding the sturdy handle of a large black suitcase in one long-fingered hand. The lightly scuffed leather matched his stack-heeled boots, while the rest of him was clad in faded denim.

Still trying to get her bearings, Abby closed the rust-colored door behind him. She would have liked to lean against it, at least long enough to shut her eyes for an instant and draw in a steadying breath. Instead, she squared her shoulders, knowing full well that she had to deal with her visitor—good Lord, he was about to become a guest!—and her nerves would have to wait. Ready or not, it was time to assume her hostess duties, and she could only hope this particular visit would be short.

"Welcome to Harmony, Arizona," she said, calling up the most politely offhand tone she could muster.

"Thanks." He left it at that before he followed her toward a makeshift front desk to one side of the center oak staircase. No trivial conversation, she couldn't help but note. No easy chuckles, either. Not the barest hint of the breezy charm that had seemed almost second nature to the man she'd known.

Abby groped to take in those facts and found herself frowning as the smarts she usually put to good use finally kicked in. Although she remained more than a little at sea after the shock she'd just been treated to, it was becoming increasingly clear, at least to her way of reasoning, that no one could appear so entirely indifferent to another person they had shared so much with.

It wasn't normal. And neither, she was more than beginning to suspect, was this situation.

Abby's frown deepened with each step forward. The man who had just arrived, the same one currently following hard on her heels, wasn't putting on an act and pretending not to recognize her. She was all but positive of that now, mainly because there wasn't the slightest reason to believe otherwise. In any case, it would have taken a world-class actor to pull it off. And since there was also no way she could have slipped his mind, surely not after their joint and hardly casual history, she was left to come to one conclusion.

Ryan Larabee honestly and truly didn't have a clue as to who she was. As far as he was concerned, she *was* a stranger. Which could only mean that something was wrong, Abby told herself as she made her way around the small butterscotch-colored desk standing on thin, gracefully curved legs.

Yes, something had to be very wrong.

RYAN GLANCED AROUND HIM as his hostess completed the necessary paperwork to check him in, wondering if he'd ever been in a place like this before. A gingerbread house—that had been his first impression as he'd stood on a narrow sidewalk backed by a tree-lined street and viewed the large, frame home painted a bright cinnamon with rusty-red trim around gleaming windows. Strange, he knew what a gingerbread house was, could even picture a layer of white frosting decorating a pitched roof, but whether he had ever taken a bite out of one was a total mystery.

He could only damn well hope that situation would change, and soon.

"Your room is at the top of the stairs to the right, first door on the left."

Ryan nodded in response to the soft yet briskly issued statement. He had to admit he'd expected at least a slightly warmer and less strictly business-like welcome than he'd gotten so far at Aunt Abigail's. He'd been told that Harmony, set in a valley rimmed by low, pine-dotted mountains northeast of Phoenix and offering plenty of crisp sunshine, wasn't just a great spot to visit location-wise, it was also a place that prided itself on its friendliness.

Friendly? For a minute there, waiting on the threshold, he'd discovered himself questioning whether the woman answering the merry doorbell would let him in at all.

Not that it had been a hardship to watch her do a decent job of staring him down with a smoky-green gaze. She was easy on the eyes, no doubt about it. If a man were partial to redheads of the tall and willowy variety, not precisely beautiful yet with skin that looked as smooth as cream, she'd fit the bill.

Something told him he was that kind of man, and it wasn't his brain talking. No, it was his body that was letting him know in no uncertain terms exactly what sort of woman attracted him.

"A buffet breakfast is available between seven and nine-thirty, and the front door is locked for the night at ten o'clock. If you plan to be out later than that—"

"Why, of course, he plans to be out later, at least on occasion," another soft voice, this one bubbling with good cheer, offered just then. The well-rounded woman it belonged to, one currently bustling her way down the hall from the rear of the house, might have had Everyone's Favorite Grandmother stitched across the ruffled top of her pearly white apron. Silvery hair caught up in a high bun and sparkling gray eyes only enhanced the image.

"If this is Mr. Larabee," she added, "which I assume it is, he'll be here for a while. Too long for a young man to go to bed with the birds every night, I'm sure.''

His hostess hesitated a second before countering that statement with her own, one issued in a tone more blunt than cheerful. ''You only wrote tonight's date down in the register.''

''With a little dash after it, dear.'' Standing at one side of the desk, the older woman pointed with a short and what seemed to be flour-dusted finger. ''That means this particular guest wasn't certain about the length of his visit.''

''Hmm.''

She wasn't overjoyed at that news, Ryan noted. But if the redhead's companion noticed it as well, she ignored the evidence and fixed him with a sunny smile. ''I'm Ethel Freeman, and I do hope you'll enjoy your stay here, Mr. Larabee.''

''I answer to Ryan,'' he said, dredging up a smile of his own. He doubted it was half as effective as hers, but he hadn't had much practice smiling lately.

''Yes, of course,'' she continued, barely missing a beat. ''Please call me Ethel. I'm sure Abby will want to be on a first-name basis, too. It's always so much more comfortable.''

Comfortable was the last thing the woman with the deep russet hair appeared to be at the moment, but Ryan decided to do some ignoring himself. Could be that something about him bothered her, or maybe it was just men in general. Either way, hanging around right now probably wouldn't win him any points.

He took a quick step back from the desk, grateful that his muscles readily responded even though a tight group stretching down one of his thighs was starting to give him hell. "I'll take up my bag," he said, "and get settled in. Can you recommend a place for dinner tonight?"

Abby, as he guessed he should call her, opened her mouth, only to snap it shut again when Ethel wasted no time in saying, "Since it's your first night here and you're the only guest, weekdays in spring usually being a slower time, why don't you have dinner with us? I'm making one of my favorites—chicken and dumplings."

He had no idea if he shared a fondness for that dish, but it sounded good. And, although he was well aware that Abby hadn't hurried to second the invitation, not by any means, he was tired enough to give in without hesitation. "Sounds terrific. What time do we eat?"

"Six o'clock," Ethel promptly informed him. "The dining room is off the hall toward the back of the house, on the left."

"I'll be there." And with that he picked up his luggage and started toward the stairs, doing his damnedest not to limp, not while an audience was around. A man had his pride, after all, and he didn't care what the doctors said about mustering some patience for the healing process.

At least certain other parts of him appeared to be in full working order. Ryan smiled again, this time to himself. He'd been worried on that score, he had to admit. But not any longer. All it had taken was the sight of one particular long-legged, green-eyed, smooth-skinned female to have him dead sure that he was in top-notch shape in one very important area. No matter what, he was still a red-blooded male.

From a short distance below him, the woman in his

thoughts watched him climb the steps. She didn't miss the way he seemed to favor one leg over the other, but probably only because her currently heightened senses were so attuned to his every move. Whatever the case, there was no denying the strength of the arm carrying the hefty suitcase with ease. She might well have had to use both her arms and all her resources to accomplish the same feat.

But then, he had always been strong. Although the faded blue sleeves of his waist-high jacket hid them from view at the moment, she had no trouble recalling the sight of solidly muscled, hair-darkened forearms. Lean and powerful.

"He seems to be the quiet sort," Ethel remarked, still at Abby's side.

Not hardly, was the first thought to surface. Then again, Abby told herself, maybe that was true now. Maybe partying well into the night no longer occupied a prominent place on his list of favorite things to do. Maybe.

One thing was for sure, as much as he'd once enjoyed a good party, how he earned his living had always been so high on his personal list that it regularly trounced everything else competing for his time and attention. It was difficult—almost impossible—to believe that would ever change, no matter what had happened to him since they'd parted ways.

As for the immediate future, Abby knew there was little she could do about the fact that they would be seeing each other frequently. She'd committed to remaining here until the end of May, which was still weeks away, and commitments were important enough to her to have her vowing to see this one through, regardless of how long a certain guest chose to stay.

"Such a nice name," Ethel said. "Ryan Larabee."

"I suppose so." Abby's tone was staunchly neutral.

Ethel sighed softly. "Has a romantic ring to it, don't you think?"

"Hmm." She'd once thought exactly that, Abby silently admitted. But that was before she'd firmly set romance aside, leaving it to those who were still starry-eyed. She valued other things in a relationship now, like mutual interests and comfortable companionship. Both of which she felt she'd found with—

Another sigh broke into that reflection, this one long and heartfelt. "Oh, if only I were forty years younger and fifty pounds lighter."

Abby had to grin. "Oh, if only I could cook like you. I wouldn't even mind gaining some weight in the effort."

Ethel beamed. "Thank you, dear. Even though they're mostly grown, my grandchildren still seem to favor my baking when I visit them in California. And speaking of children, what time is the little darling due up from her nap?"

Abby glanced at her thin gold wristwatch, a gift from her parents on her last birthday. It was elegant enough to win notice, yet in the best of conservative taste—much like the couple who had produced her. "The little dickens," she said, "should be up soon enough that I'd better check on her. Yesterday afternoon, she was standing at the side of the crib, holding on to the railing for all she was worth and getting ready to let everyone within yelling distance know she was awake."

This time, Ethel's smile was fond. "You're doing a good job in the mothering department, I have to say."

"I'm going to give it everything I've got," Abby replied, and fully meant it. Although the role had been thrust on her after the heartbreaking loss of two dear friends, she was determined to fill it to the best of her ability.

Years earlier she had very much wanted children. Then, when her life had been turned upside down while she was still in her early twenties, she had concentrated on building a career in Arizona's flourishing resort industry. Now she was, in every sense other than having given birth, a mother. And motherhood, she'd already discovered, was as challenging as anything she'd tackled on the business front.

Abby tucked her ivory silk blouse more firmly into the waistband of her beige slacks and started for the stairs. She didn't want to think about the man who had climbed them only moments ago, didn't doubt for an instant that it would be far easier, and definitely more satisfying, to consider the child about to wake up, the one who had won a big chunk of her heart.

Then, too, she reflected, there was someone else who deserved consideration, a great deal of it. After all, not every woman had an attractive doctor in her life. She'd never expected to have one, either, until recently. Her parents had been heartily pleased by that development, her godmother unfortunately less so. But he was there, nonetheless.

Abby nodded. Yes, she had a lot to consider besides the one person in her past she'd be light years better off not wasting another thought on. Reason told her that, and being the sensible, practical woman she'd made of herself since they'd last seen each other, she fully agreed.

Trouble was, she still couldn't block him out, not entirely. Especially when a niggling voice in the back of her mind kept repeating a silent question.

What in the world was wrong with him?

"THERE'S NOTHING WRONG with you, Larabee," Ryan muttered to himself as he made his way down a long hall wallpapered in narrow raspberry-and-cream stripes. His booted feet made little noise on the chocolate-brown carpet.

Thankfully, he was moving more smoothly and with less effort after he'd judged the cozy bed in his room to be too tempting and had settled for an over-stuffed chair as a good spot to rest his leg for a couple of hours. Even if he hadn't managed to completely disguise a limp earlier, nobody in the gingerbread house knew his recent injuries went beyond a bum leg, and he planned to keep it that way.

The last thing he wanted was any more people aiming concerned looks his way and asking how he felt. He'd had enough of that to last him a long while. Maybe forever.

So, as far as the residents of Aunt Abigail's were concerned, there was nothing wrong with him. Not a blasted thing. That was his story, and he was sticking to it.

Ryan reached an arched doorway, one he immediately took for his destination from the smells wafting toward him and tempting his appetite. He was hungry, and still tired from the drive that morning, he had to admit. He stepped into the room, thinking that it wouldn't be much of a problem to make small talk during dinner and excuse himself as soon as courtesy allowed.

What he found waiting for him, though, had him coming to a halt long before he reached the round oak table covered with a lacy cloth and holding center stage under an antique brass chandelier.

"Pap!"

A baby, not a newborn but probably not more than a year old, either, as far as Ryan could judge—and a girl, he decided, based on the frilly pink headband restraining a riot of dusky curls—stared straight at him with wide dark eyes. "Pap!" she shouted again from her seat in a high chair painted snowy-white, holding her short, chubby arms out in greeting.

Obviously, Ryan thought, he was *Pap*. At least she figured he was. And how did he handle that?

The grandmotherly Ethel came to his rescue. "No, Cara," she said gently from her chair set at one side of the baby's place. "This is Mr. Larabee, but we've already agreed that he'll be Ryan." She leaned in and nudged back a tiny stuffed horse in grave danger of falling off the high chair's tray. "Can you say Ryan?"

"Pap!" the small, sturdily built person named Cara didn't hesitate to repeat, eyes still locked on him.

"I think she means *Pops*," his flame-haired hostess remarked from the baby's other side. "The woman who sometimes takes care of her has two young children of her own, and that's what they call their grandfather. Pops."

"Great. Just what I need," Ryan mumbled under his breath. "Thirty-four years old and taken for somebody's granddaddy."

"I'm sorry. She's just started talking enough to

make out real words,'' the redhead said, ''and sometimes the strangest things come out.'' Rather than
look at him while offering that apology, she kept her
gaze on the baby.

Her baby? He had to wonder. He might have easily
assumed that was the case, except their coloring was
so different.

And what about a husband? She wore no ring on
the relevant finger; he'd already checked that out
while she was checking him in.

Whatever the case, it was hardly his place to ask,
and no further information was offered on either question. Instead, with the baby's attention on the task of
tearing a dinner roll apart, the conversation took a
different turn altogether.

He'd taken a seat and a large china plate filled to
the brim was set in front of him, when Ethel inquired
politely, ''What part of the country do you come
from, Ryan? That is, if you don't mind my asking.''

He didn't mind. This was part of the small talk he'd
anticipated, and that he could handle. *Stick to the basics, Larabee,* he told himself, *and you'll be okay.*

''Wyoming, originally,'' he replied, grateful to be
sure on that score. Studying a copy of his personnel
file while he was still laid up in the hospital had provided some essential information. ''More recently,
I've been living in southern Arizona.''

Ethel's mouth curved up at the tips. ''Why am I
getting the feeling that you're a cowboy?''

A cowboy? On the outside, maybe. The clothes in
his closet said he favored the trappings. But in practice? He knew the answer to that one.

Ryan shook his head. ''Actually, I'm a pilot.'' He
hesitated before deciding it wouldn't hurt to add,

"For the past few years, I've flown a helicopter for the Border Patrol."

Abby blinked at that news. She set her fork down carefully and reached for her water glass, hoping she didn't look as interested as she couldn't help being.

He'd flown freelance for a living during the time she'd known him. That he'd gone to work for a government agency surprised her a little. He hadn't been fond of structure of any type. But it didn't surprise her, not a whit, that he'd continued to fly.

If he had quit, she would have been stunned.

"Land sakes," Ethel replied, eyes widening. "The Border Patrol. That must be exciting."

"I suppose you could say so," Ryan said.

And that was all he said, although Abby waited, ears alert, for more. This was something new, she couldn't deny. He'd never been reluctant to talk about his work. In fact, it had been much the opposite.

She was still mulling that over when he shifted in his seat and directed a comment squarely at her. "You said this was your godmother's place."

"Mmm-hmm." She left it at that, deciding he wasn't the only one who could be tightfisted when it came to handing out information. After all, she didn't owe him any explanations. She didn't, in fact, owe him anything.

"Are you helping her run things around here?" he went on in the next breath.

"At the moment."

"Because she's away," he added, a reference to her earlier disclosure when he'd first appeared on the doorstep. "Will she be gone long?"

"No."

"Vacation?" A probing glint lit in his gaze with

that last question. Plainly her brief replies had roused his curiosity.

"Something like that," she said mildly.

And now Ethel's bright voice broke in. "Goodness gracious, dear, it's no secret that she's on her honeymoon."

Ryan's brows climbed. "Your godmother just got married?"

Abby nodded. "For a second time."

Ethel chuckled. "And for her second trip to the altar, she picked an old cowboy."

"Pap!" Cara suddenly exclaimed, again fixing the man across the table from her with a firm stare.

This time a wince crossed his face. Abby caught it and almost laughed out loud, despite everything.

"The darling reminds me of my first and so far only little great-granddaughter," Ethel said. "Gets something in her head and just won't give it up."

"Terrific," Ryan muttered, and went back to his dinner.

ABBY FOUND HERSELF tossing and turning in the middle of the night, which hardly amazed her. The day had, without a doubt, provided her nerves with a challenge, although at least dinner had gone easily enough once Ethel began to do most of the talking, treating her companions to a short history lesson on Harmony's early beginnings when, as Ethel had put it, "a group of settlers from back East got as far as this valley in their horse-drawn wagons, took a long look around them and were smart enough to dig in their heels."

Meanwhile their guest had concentrated on his meal, doing justice to it before leaving them to head back to his room—a room Abby couldn't help but be grateful was nowhere near hers. Thank goodness for big houses.

Abby released a lengthy breath and listened to an owl hoot somewhere in the distance as she turned on her side. In contrast, not a whisper of sound came through the connecting door to the smaller room next to hers. Cara at least, snug in her crib, was getting a good night's rest. Which hadn't always been the case. Their first months together had left them both heavy-eyed in the mornings more often than not, but that seemed to be behind them. One more thing to be grateful for, Abby reflected.

Actually her blessings were many. If they didn't include getting a single wink of sleep tonight, she would still count herself fortunate.

Was *he* getting any sleep?

The question slipped into her mind as she closed her eyes and settled deeper into the pillow. The answer shouldn't matter to her one way or the other. And it didn't, she assured herself. But she couldn't help wondering.

As far as the accommodations went, she knew that any guest at Aunt Abigail's should find a peaceful night's rest easy to achieve. The rooms, although not especially large by conventional hotel standards, had nevertheless been furnished with care. Dotted-swiss curtains, bright ceramic lamps and chintz-covered lounging chairs provided a homey touch. Plus, to make things even more comfy, most of the rooms on the guest half of the second floor featured the coziest of feather—

Abby's eyes popped open to stare up into the darkness as another memory surfaced, one she'd totally forgotten. Until now.

Ryan Larabee was allergic to certain types of feathers, particularly those often used in bedding material. And the room she'd given him had all of the comforts many visitors found so much to their liking…including a plump feather bed.

In the normal course of events, he would have immediately said something about it. Instead he'd said not one word—because he didn't remember that allergy any more than he remembered her. It was the only conclusion she could come to, and now knowing full well what he apparently didn't, she supposed she had to do something.

Of course, you have to, her conscience said, in no uncertain terms.

Abby swallowed a sigh, tossed back the covers and got to her feet, sending the long skirt of her emerald silk nightgown plunging to her ankles. She pulled on a matching robe, belted it tightly around her waist, and shoved her toes into ivory satin slippers. Making a midnight visit to a certain man's room was the last thing—the very last thing—she wanted to do.

Having a healthy conscience, she decided grimly, could be a definite liability.

She slipped quietly from her room, made her way down the carpeted hall that ran crosswise from one side of the house to the other, opened the door that divided the family area from the guest quarters, and had scarcely reached the first room past the center staircase when a muffled sneeze shattered the silence.

Now she absolutely had to go through with it.

She drew in a breath and knocked softly on a creamy-white door, telling herself that she was prepared for whatever greeted her. Seconds later she stood facing a bare-chested male wearing nothing more than hip-hugging denim, and for the second time in less than twenty-four hours she could only stare. No matter what her brain had to say on the subject, her eyes were determined to look their fill. And they did.

It took another sneeze to jolt her back to the matter at hand and have her gaze quickly rising to meet red-rimmed eyes that were still amazingly blue.

"Sorry if my hacking woke you," he said in a voice not only low but hoarse as he raised a hand and brushed back strands of dark hair hanging down his forehead. "I must have caught a cold or something."

She shook her head. "No, it's not that," she told him. "We have to change your room. You're having an allergic reaction."

A puzzled frown formed as she watched. "I'm allergic to the room?"

"To the feather bed, actually." She cleared her throat delicately. "I mean, that might well be the case," she added as reasonably as she could manage. "Some people do have an allergy to certain types of feathers."

It was his turn to stare for a silent moment before his frown deepened. "You didn't say I *might* be allergic a second ago. You said I was." His eyes narrowed. "How the devil would you know that?"

His tone was terse enough to have her chin lifting. Not only had she been trying to help him, she'd also been attempting to do it as tactfully as possible, for all the good it had done her. Well, so much for that effort, she decided, squaring her shoulders. She was through tiptoeing around something they probably should have gotten straight hours earlier.

"I know," she said very deliberately, "because I remembered just minutes ago your mentioning the allergy in question when we encountered a couple of down-filled pillows during our honeymoon."

His jaw dropped like a stone before he snapped it shut and opened it again. "*Our* honeymoon."

She nodded just once, and kept it brisk. "That's right. Maybe you don't recall me, but I happen to be your ex-wife."

Chapter Two

His wife. Ryan stood stock-still while his mind groped to take it in. His first thought was that it couldn't be. His personnel file had indicated nothing about a wife. No one he'd talked to since the accident had so much as mentioned a wife. For God's sake, he couldn't have a wife!

Then again, she'd said *ex*-wife, he reminded himself. At least he could remember that much. Belatedly, at any rate.

"When exactly were we on this honeymoon?" he managed to get out before another huge sneeze racked him.

His companion arched a tawny brow. "I think we'd better continue this discussion elsewhere, after we find you another room."

"Right." He reached up and rubbed an eye, damn thankful that his hand was still steady.

She started to turn, then swung back to him, catching her bottom lip between her teeth. "Uh, now that I think about it, none of the other rooms on this side of the house is available at the moment. Ethel's got them torn apart for the cleaning service to do their thing tomorrow so we can have them ready for more guests due to arrive this weekend.'' She hesitated. ''There is a spare room available in the family area that I suppose you could use. It's at the other end of the hall.''

Probably close to her own, he couldn't help thinking. Maybe that was why she seemed far from pleased at the prospect of letting him sleep there. Whatever the case, right now he didn't care whether she was thrilled or not. He wanted to get going and get some answers.

Ryan crossed the room in his bare feet, snatched the shirt he'd worn earlier from the chair and pulled it on, leaving it to hang open, then grabbed his wallet from an old dresser painted sunny yellow and stuffed it in a back jeans pocket. Since he'd been sleeping in no more than his skin, he figured he was set for the night. ''Let's get out of here.''

After another second's pause, she dipped her head in a nod. ''Okay. I'll show you where the spare room is, and then we can talk downstairs. I could use a cup of tea.''

''I could use a stiff drink,'' he didn't hesitate to counter as he shut the door behind him with a soft thud and followed her down the hall.

''Well then, you're in luck. My godmother's new groom keeps a small stock of beer that's touted to be Colorado's finest in the refrigerator.''

''Sounds good,'' he had to admit.

''I thought it would,'' she told him, tossing the words over her shoulder. ''Especially to you.''

He frowned. ''Why especially to me?''

She marched ahead, spine ramrod straight, her robe swishing as she walked. ''Because you were partial to that brand of beer at one time, particularly when you were in the mood to throw a party. Which, trust me, was often.''

He didn't take that as a compliment. ''How often?''

''Often enough to have the neighbors longing for some peace and quiet.''

HE WAS STILL mulling over that zinger when they faced each other across a butcher-block table set at one side of a large kitchen that was a study in contrasts, the chief of them being an old-fashioned black stove that stood next to a modern stainless-steel refrigerator. The red-and-white checkered floor looked to be far from new despite a waxy sheen, but the gleaming dishwasher set under the cocoa-colored counter and beside a porcelain sink was another story.

Ryan took a lengthy swallow from an ice-cold bottle and placed it on the table. He was more than ready for some firm facts, ones that went beyond his past partying habits. Now that the shock had worn off enough to consider a few things, he found he had no doubt about his having once been intimately involved with the woman sitting across from him sipping her tea. His body, he thought, had recognized her right off and responded accordingly. At this very moment, he knew his eyes would have found it no hardship to wander over the silky green fabric covering her breasts. Breasts that he must once have done more than look at. Yes, indeed. He had no doubt about that, either. He'd have done a lot more than look.

Haul in your libido, Larabee. It's past time to get a few answers.

Ryan reclined in the ladder-back chair and crossed his arms over his chest. ''As I asked between sneezes upstairs, exactly when were we on this honeymoon?''

Abby set her delicate china cup down on a matching saucer. "You're not questioning that we did in fact have one?"

"Not at the moment," he replied, and left it at that.

"Well then, whether you choose to believe it happened or not, we met in Tucson nearly seven years ago, in the lounge area of a restaurant near the University of Arizona where some of my friends and I were celebrating the fact that we'd graduated from U of A earlier that day. You asked me to dance. I accepted. It was pretty much a whirlwind courtship. We eloped on a scorching hot day in July, got married at a small wedding chapel on our way south, and honeymooned in Mexico."

He didn't move a muscle as he absorbed that information. "And when did we part company?"

"Barely a year later."

"Not one of the longest marriages on record," he said.

Her lips, moistly pink despite no trace of makeup, twisted. "I suppose that sums it up."

"Who wanted the divorce?"

She looked him straight in the eye. "I did."

Why? He caught the thought back before he could voice it. Something told him he wasn't going to like the answer. "And we haven't seen each other for six years?"

"No contact at all since we left the courthouse in Tucson. We had no major joint assets, like a home, and with no children involved, there was little reason to keep in touch."

He lifted a hand and ran it through his hair. "At least that explains why you weren't listed in my personnel file. I joined the Border Patrol five years ago.

They'd have done a background check at the time, but they wouldn't have been looking for ex-wives.'' And he must've kept mum about the brief marriage when it came to his fellow agents, he thought to himself. They might be nearly as amazed to learn what he had just discovered as he'd been. As for where his copy of the marriage—not to mention divorce—papers were, he'd come across a key for a safe deposit box, one he hadn't checked out yet.

''The personnel records showed my parents as deceased,'' he added, ''and a sister living in Wyoming as next-of-kin.''

''Mmm-hmm. Have you spoken to her?''

''No, not yet.'' That was something else he'd been meaning to do. ''If I *had* contacted her, she'd probably have broken the news before you rocked me back on my heels with it.''

''She might have mentioned me,'' Abby agreed. ''Certainly she knew I had joined the family. We talked on the phone a few times and exchanged Christmas cards one year. I wanted to visit her and you said we would, but we never got around to it. You always seemed to be too busy. Back then you were working as a freelance pilot, and you loved your job.''

''More than I loved to party?'' he couldn't help asking in a tone as dry as dust.

''Yes,'' she replied calmly. ''Freelance work seemed to suit you to a T. I'd ask why you gave it up...but I bet you don't know, do you?''

It was his turn to meet her gaze head-on. ''No.''

Abby leaned forward and propped her elbows on the table, deciding it was time she asked some questions. Especially one. ''What happened, Ryan?''

After a second's hesitation, he heaved a gusty sigh. "Unfortunately, I'm not real clear on that subject. The first thing I remember is coming to on a flat stretch of desert a few miles north of the border with the wind howling in my ears. I was strapped into a helicopter that was a lot worse for wear. Apparently I'd set it down during one devil of a spring dust storm—or maybe crash-landed would be a better description."

God, he might have been killed. That was all she could think. A chill ran down Abby's spine at the realization of just how close he'd probably come to total disaster.

"I drifted in and out of consciousness. Mostly out, I imagine. The next thing I knew, a state highway cop was looking me straight in the eye and asking who I was." Ryan chuckled, but the sound held no humor. "I guess it was a helluva shock to both of us when I had to tell him I didn't have a clue."

Abby frowned. "You don't remember anything at all?"

He shook his head. "Not about *me*. The only way I can explain it is that I have no trouble recalling the mechanics of how to drive, but what kind of cars I've driven in the past are another thing altogether."

"What do the doctors say?"

He lifted a broad shoulder in a shrug. "That it could all come back to me tomorrow. Then again, it might take a lot longer than that. Head injuries are apparently chancy. One thing for dead sure, people in white coats have done enough poking and prodding to last me a lifetime."

The clipped edge to that last comment told her he'd be happy to drop the subject. She could understand why, too. It had to be frustrating beyond belief to have no idea when the memories would return, or even if they would, totally. And he'd injured more than his head. Now she knew the reason for the slight limp she'd caught earlier. "How's your leg?" she inquired mildly.

A rueful expression crossed his face. "I guess I didn't fool you, huh?"

"You nearly did," she told him. "It wasn't that noticeable."

"I don't notice it much myself anymore," he said. "It was probably the long drive this morning that did it. The muscles seem to knot up when I'm sitting too long."

"You drove up from Douglas?" she asked, recalling the address he'd given as his residence when he'd checked in.

"Uh-huh."

The location had made sense to her once he'd revealed his current government employer. Douglas, a smaller city at Arizona's southern tip, was much closer to the border than Tucson. But both were a long way from where he was now. And that brought up another question. "Why did you come to Harmony?"

He met it with a question of his own. "Do you know a guy named Jordan Trask?"

She shook her head.

"He used to be with the Border Patrol before he moved here. He called me yesterday after hearing about the accident from someone else we both worked with down south. Trask didn't waste any time in suggesting that I get away for a while and give this town a try." Ryan grimaced wryly. "Actually, he flat-out ordered me to get my butt in gear and haul myself up here. Said this place would make a new man of me.''

Abby had to smile. ''Sounds like he might be a good friend to have.''

''I can't argue with that. He says we've known each other for as long as I've been with the agency.''

But Ryan didn't remember him, any more than he remembered her. Or anyone else. She couldn't help but feel more than a little sympathy, yet she held back on expressing any, suspecting it would not be welcome. ''Did he tell you about Aunt Abigail's?''

''Yeah.'' This time his low chuckle held some genuine humor. ''He stayed here at one point, even raved about the feather beds.''

She laughed and found it felt good, despite everything. ''You'll have to thank him.''

''I will, believe me. I plan on paying him a visit this weekend.''

Abby took another sip of tea. ''So you're staying in Harmony for a while?'' The question was as casual as she could make it.

He nodded. ''I'm in no hurry to head south again. Actually the people I work for don't seem in any rush to have me back on the job. They keep telling me to get a good rest. It's pretty clear that at least some of the powers-that-be consider me a loose cannon right now.'' He blew out a disgusted breath. ''It's like I lost my mind instead of my memory. If this drags on, they'll probably agree to give me a desk job, where they can keep an eye on me while I push papers around, but I won't be doing any flying for them as things stand, that's plain.''

There was no hint of anguish in his last remark. None. And that surprised her. ''Won't you miss it?''

"The flying?" His expression turned thoughtful. "I don't know. I haven't missed it yet, not especially. It's the inactivity, the doing nothing besides coddling myself, that's beginning to drive me up the wall."

Now Abby was stunned clear down to her toes. Good Lord. *He hadn't missed it.*

Blue eyes narrowed in suspicion. "You don't think I'm crazy, too, do you?"

"Ah, no, of course not."

"Then why are you goggling at me?"

She was, she abruptly realized, and made herself stop. "I'll admit to being a little amazed," she said after a moment, well aware that was a gross understatement. "Flying was once as important to you as breathing."

The sheer truth was, Abby thought, flying had been more important to him than anything. Everything. Including her. Once she'd accepted that, she'd known their marriage was in major trouble.

"Could be it was exactly as you say," he allowed. "Right now, though, it's as foggy as everything else. If I had to do it this second, I don't think I'd have any bigger problem figuring out how to fly than I did how to drive. But how it felt to be a pilot is another story. It's one more piece of the past behind this damned blank wall in my mind." His jaw tightened. "The whole thing is bugging me, I don't deny it. That's another reason I'm in no hurry to go back south. I'd just wind up roaming around my apartment and muttering to myself."

"You live alone?" Again she tried for a casual tone, and knew she hadn't succeeded when his eyes lit with a knowing gleam.

"As a matter of fact, I do. Apparently, there's been

no woman in my life lately.'' He paused for two ticks of the kitchen clock. ''Who do you live with?''

''Cara,'' she replied without hesitation. ''We're currently living in my condo in Phoenix.'' But not for too much longer, Abby thought with satisfaction. By the time Cara was a toddler, they'd be settled into a real home, one with a backyard big enough for a little girl to play in to her heart's content.

And it wouldn't be just the two of them.

''Is she your baby, or have you adopted her?''

That question brought Abby up short. Then again she supposed she shouldn't be startled to learn that he thought she might be Cara's birth mother. She could have had several children in the years since they'd parted.

So could he.

But she didn't think that was the case. In fact, if he were to confess to becoming a father during those same years, she knew it would amaze her every bit as much as his statement that he hadn't missed being able to fly.

No, she was the one who had taken on the role of parent. Or, rather, fate had given it to her.

''Cara is the only child of a couple I considered two of my best friends,'' Abby explained. ''I met Elena, Cara's mother, in college. Elena had huge dark eyes, mounds of curly black hair, and more than her share of ambition. She moved to the Phoenix area after we graduated and made her mark in the business world before marrying. Like Elena, her husband was a product of the foster-care system and had to overcome some real challenges in order to succeed in life. After I moved to Phoenix myself several years ago, I saw them on a regular basis, and they asked if they

could name me as Cara's guardian in the event anything happened to them. I agreed, although none of
us expected anything to happen, not as young as they
were. But it did.'' Abby's sigh was long and heartfelt.
''They lost their lives in a boating accident on Lake
Pleasant when Cara was nine months old.''

''That's tough,'' Ryan said soberly.

''Yes,'' she agreed, her voice quiet. ''Since then
I've started formal adoption proceedings, which
should go smoothly, given that her parents offered me
that choice in their wills.''

Abby got up and rinsed her cup in the sink, then
turned back to the man still seated at the table. A man
who looked entirely too good with his shirt hanging
open and his bare feet sticking out from the table. A
man who had always looked too good for his own
good. And hers.

''So you and the kid are going back to Phoenix?''
Ryan said, echoing the casual tone she'd aimed for
earlier. Something made her wonder if it was as bogus
as hers had been.

''At the end of the month,'' she replied.

''I suppose you have a job there?''

''I did until recently.'' Abby leaned against the
counter. ''I was an assistant manager at a major resort
hotel, but that didn't leave enough time or energy to
deal with my new responsibilities, and I decided Cara
came first.''

He lifted his beer for another swallow. ''So you
plan on being a full-time mother?''

''For the moment. I can work part-time in a less
demanding job when she's a little older and I'm sure
she's settled.'' Abby's lips curved gently. ''We had

some hurdles to cross during our first months together, but we both came through fine.''

"Well, that baby may have me mixed up with somebody's granddaddy, but she looks healthy enough,'' Ryan allowed. "Maybe you should get her eyesight checked, though.''

Abby swallowed a laugh. "I think her eyes are fine. And as for the rest of her, she has a handsome pediatrician who plans to make sure she stays healthy.''

As if he'd sensed something in that last comment, Ryan slowly straightened in his chair. "Dedicated man?'' he asked, lifting a brow.

"Definitely.''

Abby pushed away from the counter and started for the door to the hall. She knew she didn't need to expand on that, knew it was none of Ryan Larabee's business what she planned on doing with her life, knew she'd probably be better off just going back to bed and leaving him without another word. None of that stopped her from halting in the doorway and aiming a look over her shoulder. She simply couldn't resist.

"Not only dedicated,'' she added with determined good cheer, "but excellent father material. That's why I had to seriously consider his offer when he asked me to marry him.''

Ryan stilled completely. His gaze locked with hers. "What,'' he asked softly, "did you tell him?''

"I said yes.''

WELL, SO WHAT if she planned on marrying a baby doctor? It was none of his concern, Ryan reminded himself as he made his way back to the kitchen the following morning. He had plenty of his own concerns, the chief one being the need for something to jump-start his system before he did a round of the daily exercises the physical therapist had recommended.

Another damned doctor type.

Ryan passed the dining room, currently empty except for the gracefully aging furniture taking up most of it, and found Everyone's Favorite Grandmother in the kitchen, wearing another ruffled apron and humming what sounded like a classic rock-and-roll tune as she stood at the stove. Rock and roll? Nah, he decided as he stopped in the doorway. "I know it's not quite breakfast time, but do you think I could beg a cup of coffee?"

Ethel turned and beamed a smile his way. "Well, of course, Ryan. Have a seat and I'll pour it for you."

"I can get it," he said, pleased to note that the coffeemaker on the counter had already done its job. "Just point me in the direction of the cups."

Ethel did, and he soon found himself seated at the kitchen table for the second time in a matter of hours. Unfortunately, Ryan thought, he hadn't managed to get much sleep after his ex-wife had waltzed out and left him with her cheerful announcement ringing in the air.

I said yes.

"Are you hungry?"

He blinked. "What?"

"I just put some buttermilk biscuits in the oven," Ethel told him. "How about a couple of farm-fresh eggs and homemade sausage to go with them?"

His stomach answered with a growl. Food had been the last thing on his mind, but the smells drifting his way from the stove had apparently changed things. "Sounds good," he had to admit.

"I do love to cook for a man with a hearty appetite."

His stomach rumbled one more time. "As it happens, Ethel, I think I can oblige you."

He was forking up a helping of eggs scrambled to perfection when Abby walked in and came to a dead halt at the sight of him. The baby she held immediately flung a sturdy little arm covered by stretchy pink terry cloth in his direction.

"Pap!"

Ryan managed not to wince, barely. "Definitely need to get those eyes checked out," he muttered under his breath.

"I think she has a crush on you," Ethel teased.

"I think she has to eat her cereal," Abby tossed in even as she resisted the urge to sigh, thinking that this man still looked entirely too good, even with his shirt buttoned and a full night's growth of beard shading his jaw. She was thankful she had traded her nightgown and robe for a sage camp shirt and khaki slacks—not exactly business attire, but, nevertheless, far from intimate.

Right now, she didn't need intimate.

"The little darling's appetite is as hearty as our guest's." That was Ethel's contention.

Abby could hardly disagree, since food was undeniably one of Cara's priorities. With that in mind, it didn't take her long to seat herself at the table with the baby in her lap. Then she settled into the job of feeding the small bundle of curiosity who, dark eyes wide with wonder, divided her attention between a quickly diminishing bowl of cereal and the man tackling his own meal with obvious enthusiasm.

Not that it was strictly routine for a visitor to be enjoying his breakfast in the kitchen, Abby reflected. Ordinarily guests were welcome to serve themselves in the dining room, where Ethel kept a lengthy oak sideboard well stocked with a variety of hot and cold dishes along with a generous supply of Aunt Abigail's special sugar-and-spice cookies.

Then again, Ryan Larabee was no ordinary guest. Abby knew that full well—and so did he, she imagined, judging by the thoughtful cast of the looks he ventured her way between bites of food and sips of coffee, as if he were wondering just what kind of wife she'd made. Or maybe, getting down to sheer basics, how she'd been as a bed partner.

Goodness knows, she had no trouble remembering how he'd been in that area. In fact, seeing him again had brought back several details she could have done without recalling. Oh, yes.

"Ma!" Cara suddenly prodded, as though reminding the woman who held her to get back to the business at hand.

Abby's heart warmed at the sound of a word she was still far from used to hearing. "Well, you got that one right, little dickens," she said, summoning a smile as she slid another spoonful into an eagerly waiting mouth. "I am your mama now, and I'm sorry I slacked off on the job."

"I think her appetite is better than mine." Ryan lifted a brow as he leaned back in his chair, coffee cup in hand, and studied the baby.

"Pap!" was Cara's response just as the kitchen phone rang.

"Aunt Abigail's," Ethel answered with brimming good cheer. "All right," she went on after a brief pause. "See you then." She hung up and looked at Abby. "The newlyweds made it back to Phoenix late last night, right on schedule. They'll be checking out of the airport hotel after breakfast and should be here in a few hours. I can't wait to hear about their cruise."

"Mmm. Me, too," Abby said, even though she wouldn't have minded waiting for something else she knew was on today's agenda. Too bad she didn't have that option, not when it came to breaking some news about the reappearance of a particular man.

Ethel had no idea who Ryan Larabee was, not really. Neither would the happy groom. But the bride was another matter. The mere mention of his name would have her godmother's ears perking up in recognition. And no more than a glimpse of him would have memories of the times they'd met flooding back. Of that Abby was positive.

Women didn't forget a man like Ryan. Even women who were old enough to be his mother. Or grandmother.

So when the newlyweds returned, she had to be ready not only to tell them that her one-time spouse had unexpectedly arrived in Harmony, but also to explain why his own past was currently a mystery to him. And then she'd probably have to explain to Ethel, who'd have to be told as well, under the circumstances, why she hadn't said something before.

Abby sighed. That was a lot of explaining.

What she didn't plan on so much as mentioning, though, was the fact that the sight of this particular male still had the power to flutter her pulse, and more than a bit. She had no intention of letting anyone in on that little secret.

Especially him.

RYAN EYED the woman with salt-and-pepper hair cut stylishly short standing in the bedroom doorway. The stranger dressed in a copper-colored pantsuit and built along slender lines had summoned him with a brisk knock seconds earlier. He couldn't help but be glad that he'd already shaved, showered and pulled on a clean shirt and jeans, because it didn't take a genius to figure out that he was being sized up by a pair of amber eyes that seemed to miss nothing.

"Good morning," he said, when she offered no greeting of her own. He held the gaze he'd had to dip his chin a sharp notch to meet, given that she was nowhere near his height. The top of her head would scarcely reach halfway up his chest. And she was probably half his weight, as well. Nevertheless, *formidable* was the first word that came to mind to describe her.

"You don't remember me, do you?" she asked abruptly, her voice soft, the question blunt.

"No," he said.

Her gaze didn't falter. "May I come in?"

He stepped back from the doorway. "Why not?"

"I suppose I should introduce myself," she told him as he shut the door behind her. "I'm Abigail Stockton, though I prefer to be called Gail." She held out a small hand. "I'm also your ex-wife's godmother."

He studied her for a moment. "It seems you've got my number," he said, keeping his tone mild as they shook hands.

"We met a long time ago," she informed him. "I wasn't a Stockton back then. I just recently became one."

"So I heard. How was the honeymoon?"

She arched a well-shaped brow. "Too short. But that's not what I came to talk about."

"Somehow I didn't think it was," he murmured dryly.

"Hmm. Why don't we sit down?"

He agreed with a nod and seated himself on the teak double bed while she sank into a leather chair set under a window flanked by ivory drapes. He'd already noted that the room where he'd spent the last half of the night bore little resemblance to the other parts of the house he'd seen so far. Heartily Homey, as he'd come to think of the cozy style, didn't rule here. He had to wonder if that was the case with all of the bedrooms on the family side of the house, including the one occupied by the woman who had once shared his name. Briefly.

"As I said," his visitor continued, "we met years ago, not long after my goddaughter began dating you."

"But before we got married," he tacked on.

"Yes." She sat back and gracefully crossed one leg over the other. "Actually, I was the one who advised her to listen to her heart, rather than to her parents' doubts about the wisdom of getting seriously involved with you."

He folded his arms over his chest. "I take it they weren't thrilled with me."

"Not much," his visitor acknowledged. "Abby's parents already had two sons well on the way to being teenagers when she was born. I think she came as something of a surprise to them, and perhaps not an entirely welcome one at the time. By then, the country-club sort of lifestyle they had worked hard to achieve was on the horizon. Howard Prentice had become a senior executive. Lillian, one of my longtime and very good friends, was busy making a place for herself and her family in Tucson society. A new baby didn't precisely fit into their plans. Nevertheless, they loved their daughter and wanted the best for her, which certainly applied to a husband.''

She pursed her lips. ''I have to confess it seems strange to be telling you all this. You were probably well aware of how they felt back then.''

''Trust me, if I was, I don't recall it. Or anything else,'' he added grimly.

Her gaze darkened. ''Abby told us about the accident,'' she said, her tone gentler.

''Us?''

''My husband. And Ethel. We don't plan on spreading it around, if you're worried about that.''

He blew out a breath. ''It's not much of a secret, anyway.'' He had no desire to dwell on the subject, though, so he said, ''Exactly where did we meet?''

''At a large party Abby's parents hosted one evening in their backyard. They were celebrating the fact that they had just moved into the house of their dreams. I drove down from Harmony for the occasion, and to see Abby, as well. Unfortunately, I never had any children of my own. Which made my godchild even more special to me, I suppose.'' She paused for a beat. ''And there you were when I arrived, grinning a wide grin at something someone had said, every inch the dashing pilot. You were quite a sight, I must admit. And not only dashing, I soon discovered, but charming, as well.''

''But not charming enough to win over the folks, huh?''

''No.'' Her eyes took on a twinkle. ''They had someone far more conservative in mind, a corporate type complete with three-piece suit. Which you definitely were not. You won me over, however, if that's any consolation. It wasn't the easy charm that did it, though. It was the way you and Abby looked at each other when you called her...''

''When I called her what?'' Ryan prompted at the hesitation, his curiosity stirred.

She shook her head. ''It's not important—and not strictly my place to tell you, when you come right down to it. The main thing is, there was the kind of spark between you two that not every couple experiences, not by any means. I felt it once when I was a much younger woman, but I married someone else, because my parents begged me to be sensible, and I listened. I'm not saying I wasn't content with my late husband. He was a good person. But contentment is no substitute for love.'' A soft smile curved her mouth. ''Luckily the man I gave up came back into my life recently and swept me off my feet.''

''That would be the cowboy Ethel mentioned.''

''Yes. His name is Bill.'' Gail's expression sobered. ''Bill and I planned to work full-time fixing up the place he bought on the outskirts of the city. Right up to the day before the wedding, that was our intention. And then everything changed.''

''Mind expanding on that?'' Ryan asked when she halted.

She ran her tongue over her lips, as if debating

whether to say more before she shrugged and went on. "My goddaughter, having already resigned from her job in Phoenix, had agreed to come up for the wedding in late April, help look after things in my absence, and then spend the rest of May here in order to give herself time to decide on becoming partners with me and managing the bed and breakfast. It would have been perfect for her. For all of us, in fact. Bill and I would be free to live out at his place, while Ethel, who needs a job, since her late husband didn't leave her much, stayed on here. And Abby would have an ideal spot in a friendly family neighborhood to raise Cara."

Ryan nodded to himself, thinking that he now had a good hunch what had scuttled the whole thing. "And then a certain doctor entered the picture."

Gail's gaze sharpened. "So she told you about—"

"The new fiancé? Uh-huh." She had, in fact, Ryan thought, relished telling him about it.

"Well, that's what happened the day before the wedding," Gail continued. "Abby phoned and asked if she could bring a guest, and then broke the news that she had just become engaged."

"Which put a huge damper on your plans," Ryan summed up.

She sighed a long sigh. "Lord, I wish it were that simple. I'd give up whatever plans I had in a heartbeat if they stood in the way of her happiness, believe me. The problem is that this man is all wrong for her."

Ryan felt his brows make a fast climb. "You mean the good doctor isn't so good?" For some reason it pleased him, more than a little, to think that the guy was a jerk.

Gail squashed that notion in the next breath. "I

mean that he's as handsome as sin and has a list of virtues an angel might well envy. Abby's parents gushed all over him at my wedding. But, as far as I'm concerned, he's still not right for her. There's no...spark.''

As there had been with him. At least he had that satisfaction, Ryan told himself, aiming his gaze past the window to look out at bright sunlight. Not that it should make any difference to him. And not that it apparently did to Abby. Whether she was engaged to the right guy or not, husband number one no longer seemed to be striking any sparks.

Or she'd gone out of her way to give that impression.

''Do you still care about her?'' Gail asked quietly, regaining his attention.

''I don't know.'' It was all he could say. ''Hell, I don't even know who I am, not really.''

But he wanted her. That much he recognized full well, especially after spending the last half of the night in a room only steps from hers and wondering how it had felt to have her stretched out under him. His body wouldn't have objected to finding out, that was certain. His brain, on the other hand, wasn't flat-out sure of anything. ''Right now, I only know who other people tell me I am—or was. Can you understand that?''

Gail shook her head. ''I don't suppose anyone could who hasn't been in your situation. I do understand, though, that I care deeply about my goddaughter. I am thankful that she's agreed to spend the rest of the month here, as planned. I can only hope she'll think long and hard about this engagement, because I would hate to see her make another mistake.'' She released another sigh. "I was once so sure you were the right man for her."

His sudden smile was wry. "Someone told me coming here would make a new man of me."

Gail rose to her feet and studied him for a long moment. "Maybe it will," she said at last with a thoughtful frown.

Chapter Three

"You ran into *who?*"

"My ex-wife," Ryan repeated to the man seated beside him on a short stack of back-porch stairs. The small two-story frame home rising behind them came complete with grassy yard and white picket fence.

"Jeez," Jordan Trask said with feeling, his hazel eyes wide. As tall as his visitor and even broader through the shoulders, he was a powerfully built man in his midthirties, and currently a stunned one.

"Came as something of a shock to me, too," Ryan slid in dryly.

Jordan blew out a breath. "I can well believe it. And you ran into her at Aunt Abigail's?"

"Actually she met me at the front door."

Ryan went on to bring his former co-worker up to speed on what had happened during his first day in Harmony, as well as the first night. Although a smile crossed the other man's face at the mention of the feather-bed episode, he listened without comment. A short time later, Ryan summed up the situation. "So I not only have a former wife who just got engaged, I have even more questions about the past than I did before I knew she existed—and not one blasted thing has come back to me since the accident.'' *Including our friendship,* he thought to himself.

As though fully conscious of what hadn't been said, Jordan's expression sobered. ''That's a damn shame.''

Ryan found himself appreciating the forthright tone of that statement more than he could say. The last thing he wanted was any more coddling. Apparently this man knew him at least well enough to know that.

''Yeah,'' Ryan agreed, slapping his palms on his denim-clad knees. ''It hasn't exactly been a picnic. What really sticks in my craw, though, is that some of the people we both worked for at one time have been looking at me sideways, as if they're not too sure I can be trusted at the moment—even though, from what I understand, I was a damn good pilot before this whole thing happened.''

''Better than good,'' his companion readily conceded. ''What you could do when it came to handling a piece of aviation equipment was downright amazing sometimes. Then again, that might be part of the problem.''

Ryan frowned. ''How's that?''

''You liked to take risks, especially in the air. Although you never said as much, I got the feeling that was at least part of why you joined the agency. Guarding the border can be a dangerous proposition just from the standpoint that no one's ever sure what's going to come down next. Some people thrive on that kind of thing. I have to say you seemed to be one of them.''

Ryan's frowned deepened. ''Do you mean I got off on putting my butt on the line?''

The question won him a low chuckle. ''Let's just

say you didn't consider your own health and well-being as much as you might have. You took chances—big ones, on occasion—and I'm fairly certain the top brass didn't always appreciate that fact. You volunteered for some of the toughest assignments and got the job done, but it wasn't always done exactly their way.''

''Hmm. I suppose my last day on the job didn't earn me any points. I not only crashed the copter, but I was apparently already off course when the storm hit.''

Jordan raised a large hand and ran it through dark hair worn just long enough to brush the collar of his black polo shirt. ''My guess would be that you were checking something out without bothering to let headquarters know first.''

Put that way, his actions didn't sound totally responsible, Ryan had to admit, if that had indeed been the case. Maybe he'd brought some of those sidelong looks on himself. It wasn't what he wanted to believe, yet he couldn't deny it made sense.

''Anyway,'' Jordan said, ''I can see why what happened that day might have upset a few folks.'' His grin was rueful. ''Following the rules was never your strong suit, flyboy.''

Flyboy. Despite everything, Ryan had to grin. ''Did I have a nickname for you, too?''

The other man chuckled again. ''Well, I can recall your calling me a wily bastard a few times when a card game went my way instead of yours.''

Ryan's grin faded. As far as his character was concerned, he was sounding like less of a Boy Scout by the minute. ''I take it I was partial to gambling even when I wasn't flying.''

"Not any more than most guys with a little time on their hands," Jordan assured him. "Lady Luck was usually with you, though, even on the ground."

And then my luck ran out, Ryan thought. These days, he couldn't dredge up a single memory of the man at his side. The truth was, the only person he felt any real connection with was the woman he'd been married to, who now planned to marry someone else. The woman who still slept just steps from him, thanks to her godmother's oh-so-casual departing comment before leaving his room that he might as well continue to use the spare bedroom on the family side of the house.

Gail Stockton had made herself scarce ever since. Ryan hadn't even got a look at her new husband yet. But something was up, he figured, because Ethel had continued to invite him to share in all of the meals she fixed, despite the fact that several other guests had arrived for the weekend.

For some reason, the decision had been made to throw him and his ex-wife together. That was the only conclusion he could come to. Not that he was complaining. He had no problem with getting more than glimpses of a certain redhead.

No, she was the one who looked a long way from pleased by the latest developments.

"I want you to know that I'd have asked you to stay with us," Jordan said, regaining his visitor's attention, "but I thought you'd need some space."

"You were right," Ryan told him, answering with the same simple directness. He wouldn't have felt comfortable, he knew, staying at the Trask home. Aunt Abigail's was a better bet.

"Which isn't to say you're not welcome to stop by at any time," Jordan added. "And I mean that."

"Thanks," Ryan replied.

"Dinner will be ready in ten minutes," a soft voice announced at that point. Jordan's wife, Tess, poked her head out the back door, her wide smile as bright as the flower-print maternity top she wore.

Her husband's gaze was frankly possessive as it settled on the woman whose honey-brown curls topped clear blue eyes. "I hope we still have some ice cream left for dessert."

She laughed. "I've been raiding the pickle jar instead."

The door shut again and Jordan looked at his guest. "We just found out that we're going to have a boy."

Ryan extended his right arm. "Congratulations," he said as they shook hands. "We've been talking so much about me that I haven't had a chance to ask what you do for a living now."

"Basically I dig in the dirt."

"What?"

Jordan grinned one more time. "I'm in the landscaping business. I'll explain how that happened over dinner." Shifting, he called, "Ali, time to go in."

A young girl Ryan had met on his arrival, Tess's nine-year-old daughter from a prior marriage, came running around the side of the house with a full-grown basset hound hard on her heels. Dressed in a striped shirt and denim overalls, she made a beeline for the man seated at Ryan's side and hopped straight into his lap, sending her brown braids swinging.

"I'm gonna eat lots tonight, Dad. I'm hungry."

"You're always hungry," he countered mildly, "just like your mother is these days." Leaning in, he pressed a smacking kiss on the top of her head. "Go wash up for dinner."

After she scrambled to her feet and went inside, the dog leading the way this time, Jordan looked at Ryan. "I've got to admit that I'm looking forward to having a son, but I still can't believe it gets any better for a man than to have a little girl around to call him Dad."

"POOP!"

Ryan came to a swift halt in the hall leading to his bedroom just as Abby appeared in the open doorway to her own room, steps behind a rapidly crawling Cara. Dressed in cartoon-character pajamas, the baby was wasting no time in heading his way after stopping him cold with a single word.

He had to hope she meant she had...pooped. And not that he was—

"Poop!" Cara repeated as she reached him. She used a tiny handful of his jeans to pull herself to a standing position, then craned her neck back as far as it would go and gazed up at him.

Cripes, she meant him.

"I thought I was Pap," he said, frowning down into a chubby-cheeked face that looked freshly scrubbed. It wasn't what he would have chosen to be called, not by a long shot, but it was better than—

"Poop!"

A muffled laugh had Ryan's gaze shifting. "I don't see what's so funny," he grumbled to the woman whose green eyes sparkled with amusement.

Abby caught her bottom lip between her teeth. "Sorry," she said after a moment. But her eyes still gleamed as she walked over to scoop up the baby.

"How did dinner with your friend go?" she asked, taking a quick step back from him.

"Fine," Ryan replied, and left it at that. What he didn't add was that he hadn't exactly been thrilled with everything he'd learned about himself during the visit.

Abby hitched Cara higher on one hip. "Ethel saved some dessert for you," she told him, the sparkle rapidly disappearing from her gaze. "She said you can have apple strudel with your breakfast, if you don't want it tonight."

It was his turn to be amused. "She likes me." *And that clearly doesn't thrill you.*

"Mmm," Abby returned in a totally neutral response as the baby babbled softly and fingered the gold-tone buttons on her silky blouse.

He'd be a lot better off keeping his mind from imagining his own fingers toying with those buttons, Ryan told himself. Which, he had to admit, might be easier to do if he wasn't positive he'd made quick work of undoing other buttons in the past. Unfortunately he was dead sure on that score, even minus his memory.

As if she might have guessed the direction of his thoughts, Abby cleared her throat. "You'll have to excuse us," she said. "It's past Cara's bedtime. We were on our way downstairs so she could say good-night to everyone."

He arched a brow. "Everyone?"

"My godmother and her husband brought over a bunch of pictures from their cruise and decided to stay for dinner. They're helping Ethel clean up."

Maybe he'd finally get to meet the new hubby, Ryan mused. It would be interesting to see what kind of man had swept such an independent woman off her feet. "Do they still plan on staying out at the groom's place?"

Abby nodded. "Until the end of the month, anyway. When I leave," she added, her voice taking on more than a hint of calm determination, "I suppose other arrangements will have to be made. Ethel can't handle everything here alone."

He crossed his arms over his chest. "Maybe not, but she can sure handle things in the kitchen." He paused for a deliberate beat. "I'm looking forward to eating lots of home-cooked meals."

She shot him a look. "Maybe we should charge you extra."

Ryan kept his expression bland, just as if he hadn't heard the irritation underscoring that statement. "Fine with me. Ethel's cooking is more than worth it. My only complaint about the food here is that I haven't had a cookie placed on my pillow since the first night."

"That's because you're sleeping in the family area now." Her thin smile held little humor. "I'm afraid you'll have to do without." And with those words she left him to make her way toward the center of the house.

Ryan kept going and entered his bedroom, planning to hang up his jacket and head downstairs himself. Instead, he crossed the room and found himself stopping by the phone on the nightstand as the urge hit to call his sister in Wyoming, something he hadn't yet done. Something he needed to do. Now. He had to wonder if she'd tell him a few other things about his character that he could have done without hearing, but whether he liked what he heard or not, he needed to find out more about the man he'd been.

The man whose wife had asked for a divorce.

A YOUNG COUPLE held hands as they walked up the steep oak staircase. Ryan nodded to them on his way down. The woman's soft laugh followed by her escort's low chuckle had him rolling his eyes. More weekend guests, he decided. And guess what they were headed upstairs to do on this Saturday night—probably in a feather bed complete with pillows sporting homemade cookies?

Sure of the answer to that one, Ryan continued on his way, thinking that Aunt Abigail's was doing a brisk business. He'd already met two other couples, both from the Phoenix area, and a retired military man from back East. All had seemed more than ready to chat. Plenty of opportunities for conversation existed, too; in addition to the dining room during breakfast hours, visitors were welcome to make themselves at home in the large living room, the adjoining library or the wide, cobblestone patio by the side flower garden.

The kitchen, located next to a downstairs bedroom that Ethel used, together with a long, glassed-in back porch were reserved for the home's permanent occupants and their personal guests. Which, Ryan reflected as he made his way down the hall toward the rear of the house, seemed to include him at the moment.

Voices drifted to him from the kitchen before he reached the doorway. Figuring the dishes had been dealt with, he expected to find a small group seated at the butcher-block table, maybe sharing another round of after-dinner coffee.

What he didn't expect to see was a deck of cards and a mound of silver coins resting in the middle of that table. Or the sight of Ethel lounging in a kitchen chair with her back to a tall curtained window, wearing what looked like baggy black sweatpants topped by a white T-shirt with bold letters slashed across the front declaring Elvis Rocks!

He had to blink before his widening gaze took in her two companions, who sat at opposite ends of the table. As though they sensed his presence, all three glanced his way.

"Oh, you're back." Ethel beamed as the man sitting on one side of her rose.

"I'd like to introduce my husband, Bill," Gail said. "Bill, this is Ryan Larabee."

Ryan walked forward and caught the hand extended toward him in a firm handshake. Bill Stockton, he noted with surprise, was only slightly taller than his bride. Still, Ryan would never have considered using the word *small* to describe the wiry-built man who seemed to be all muscle, even at the age of probably sixty. No, this guy, with his thick graying hair and assessing, whiskey-brown eyes, looked as formidable as the woman he'd swept to the altar. His scarred boots, ancient Wranglers and Western-style checked shirt that fit his lean torso like a glove only added to the image.

"Pleased to meet you," Bill offered in a low, craggy voice.

So you say, Ryan thought, probing the older man's gaze, *but you're not exactly sure of that yet.* "Likewise,'' he replied mildly, figuring it could work both ways.

"How about joining us for a little poker?" Ethel asked. "We're just getting started."

Poker? In this place? He had to blink again as he shifted his gaze to hers.

"We only play for nickels," she assured him, "so you can't lose too much."

That had a grin flirting with his mouth. He didn't think he'd lose at all. Lady Luck, he remembered being told earlier that evening, had usually been with him in the past. Trouble was, he was bound to feel like a jerk if he won any of this woman's hard-earned money.

While he debated the issue, Bill sat back down at the table. "I'll take five dollars' worth," he told Ethel, who was apparently acting as banker. She counted out a bunch of coins and slid them his way.

"Okay, I'm in," Ryan said, deciding that it wouldn't hurt to play a few hands just to be sociable. He couldn't walk away with too much in a short time. Not with nickels being used for chips.

Ethel shot him another glowing smile. "Do you want to start with five dollars, too?"

His grin broke through. "Might as well."

But he wasn't grinning an hour and a bottle of cold beer later as he watched the last of his nickels make their way into Ethel's growing stack. So much for luck, he reflected ruefully. And he hadn't been the only one adding to her pile.

"What are you, a riverboat gambler in disguise?" he asked, addressing the woman seated across from him.

Ethel chuckled. "I suppose you could view this as

a lesson in the fact that appearances can be deceiving.''

''I'll say,'' Ryan muttered. ''Elvis should've tipped me off.''

Gail joined her friend in another light chuckle as Bill got up and pulled two more beers from the refrigerator. He plunked one down beside Ryan. ''Bet you figured she was most folks' version of World's Greatest Grandma come to life. Straight out of a fairy tale,'' he said, his own thin lips twitching. ''Sugar and spice and everything nice.''

It was so in tune with what he had thought on his arrival, Ryan gave his head a wry shake. ''I guess I fell for that one.''

Ethel leaned in and patted his hand. ''No more than any other visitor. The apron seems to get them every time.''

''It goes along with the rest of the place,'' Gail explained. Her gaze still held an amused glint. ''What was your impression when you first saw it from the street?''

''A gingerbread house,'' he said slowly.

''Gets them every time,'' Ethel repeated before lifting her wineglass for a short swallow.

''Keeps them coming back, too,'' Gail said. ''That's part of what makes this operation successful. People like returning to a simpler era, if only for a few days. We provide the fantasy, along with good food and a friendly atmosphere.''

Ryan ran his tongue around his teeth. ''Aren't you afraid I'll blow your cover?''

''No.'' Gail folded her arms across the front of her stylish khaki jumpsuit. ''While you're here, we consider you one of us.'' She looked him straight in the eye. "You were, after all, related to my goddaughter at one time."

"And all of that makes you eligible for our occasional poker games." Ethel rounded up the scattered cards and started to shuffle them. "Want some more nickels?"

Ryan shrugged and reached into a jeans pocket. "I suppose I can risk another five dollars' worth."

ABBY GAVE UP on the thick novel she'd been attempting to read and rose from the wicker sofa that sported well-padded, sunflower-strewn cushions. She switched off the brass floor lamp, walked over to a wide window, and looked out at the night. The view from the back porch was one of the features she liked most about the house. Even in the near-darkness, she had little trouble making out the round stone fountain set in the center of the yard, or the tall row of pines that backed it at the far rear, their branches waving in the cool, late-spring breeze drifting down from the mountains.

She'd found herself retreating to this spot on a regular basis since her arrival in Harmony, often with a book in hand. She enjoyed a good mystery. She'd once favored stories of dashing heroes saving the day to ensure a happy ending, until she'd discovered firsthand that happy endings didn't come with lifetime guarantees. Or even one-year guarantees.

She no longer sought a dashing hero. She hadn't even been seeking a husband before she'd found herself agreeing to marry someone who seemed to share her views on romantic fantasies. Certainly neither of them had been in a hurry to explore the more intimate side of their relationship. They'd sealed their engagement with a kiss. The rest, they'd both agreed, could wait. Their trip to the altar would be slow and steady.

It would be nothing, Abby thought with satisfaction, like the last time she'd wound up there.

Nevertheless, although the subject matter had changed, reading remained one of her favorite hobbies, and she'd come to relish the challenge of figuring out who dunnit, despite the fact that tonight she hadn't been able to concentrate on the unfolding plot. Tonight, another puzzle kept nagging at her, and it all had to do with the word *fine.*

"Fine," Ryan Larabee had said when she'd asked him how dinner with his friend had gone. Why did she suspect he hadn't really meant that, not entirely?

And why couldn't she let it go? she asked herself just as the door to the house creaked open. Abby angled a glance over her shoulder and found the man she knew she shouldn't be sparing a thought for snapping it shut behind him. The man she'd deliberately avoided earlier by not stopping in the kitchen on her path to the porch after putting Cara to bed. Even with his back to the hall doorway when she'd glanced in, he'd looked all too chummy playing cards with the rest of the group.

A short study of his expression as he walked toward her, clearly visible in the moonlight slanting through the windows spanning three sides of the room, gave her a good hunch as to what had happened at the card table.

"How much did Ethel take you for?" she asked, keeping her tone light.

He stopped a few steps away and shoved his hands in his pockets. "Ten bucks. I called it quits at that point."

A brief smile tugged at her lips. "Smart move. I lost more than that my first weekend here. Ethel kept saying, 'I'm sure your luck will change, dear.'"

"Right before she batted those grandmotherly gray eyes," he added in what was clearly the voice of experience.

"Did she offer a sympathetic 'It's only money,' in the sweetest way, when you finally threw in the towel?"

"Oh, yeah." He paused for a beat. "And speaking of money, I owe you for a long-distance call to Wyoming."

Abby raised an eyebrow. "You phoned your sister?"

He nodded, his expression switching to something she couldn't quite decipher.

"How is she?" Abby had to ask.

"Fine."

There was that word again. And again, Abby suspected there was far more to it. This time, though, she had an inkling of how that conversation might have gone. "I suppose you talked about the ranch?"

"The one I grew up on? Yes. That and…other things." Ryan slowly shifted his gaze and stared out at the yard. "It seems I didn't want to hang on to my share of the place after both our parents were gone. My sister and her husband bought me out."

Abby already knew as much—it had happened before she'd met him—but she offered no comment. Instead she caught her bottom lip between her teeth and kept silent, suspecting from the thoughtful tone of his last words that he was talking at least as much to himself as to her.

"I apparently didn't have much interest in the

ranch," he said, "not after I took my first flying lesson, at any rate—which disappointed my father, since I was the only son." He paused, let out a quiet breath. "I wasn't there when he had the heart attack. I'd already left to take a job as a pilot with a small air cargo company."

Yes, his sister had told it like it was, Abby reflected. At least it fit with the information Ryan had passed along to her after they were married. His mother had died when he was still a young boy, leaving her teenage daughter to care for him while their father worked to provide a living for his family.

"Now I know why I have a hefty balance in my bank account," the man at her side continued. "It came from my half of the ranch." All at once his gaze deserted the yard and shifted back to her. "At least I didn't party it all away," he added in a voice ripe with sarcasm.

"I never said you squandered your money," she countered as mildly as she could, well aware of the sudden tension ruffling the air between them. Something was bothering him, and she didn't think her earlier comments had much to do with it. No, the recent phone call was a far more likely cause.

But why was it bothering him now? she wondered. Years ago, when Ryan had shared his family history, he'd simply stated the facts and left it at that. Why did he now seem to regret the strained relationship with his father? Or at least the way the relationship had ended, with him far from home when his father had died? Maybe regrets had always dogged him, she mused, but he'd never displayed them. Not to her.

She was still mulling those questions over when he launched a blunt one of his own.

"Why did you want a divorce?"

She should have expected it, Abby told herself. In a way, it was surprising that he hadn't asked before. Still, she didn't owe him any explanations. "I don't see any need to go into it," she said, folding her arms under her breasts. She also saw no need to open old wounds—mostly hers.

His jaw set in a stubborn line. "It was because of my job, wasn't it?" When she kept her silence, he forged on. "My sister said the same thing you did— that flying was important to me. She told me I used every spare dollar I could scrape up learning to be a pilot. It only makes sense that once I got the chance, I spent much of my time in the air. Maybe even on days when I didn't have to in order to earn a living. That was why you decided to give up on the marriage, wasn't it?"

"Basically," she acknowledged, realizing he wouldn't let it go until he won some kind of admission from her. But there was more to it than his love of soaring to the clouds, she knew. Their last confrontation, the one prompting her to finally pack up and leave, had involved something else entirely. Something she had no intention of bringing up at this point.

Abby drew in a breath, let it out slowly. "Whatever happened back then, those days are over, Ryan. Yes, you spent a great deal of them flying, but it hardly matters now."

"And what about the nights?" With that quiet question he stepped forward to close the gap between them. "Did I leave you alone then, too?"

Tension rose and shimmered in the air again, of a different sort this time. She recognized it all too well.

"No, you didn't," she conceded, in a voice not nearly as cool and collected as she would have liked. He'd moved too close to let her feign total indifference. Close enough to have certain memories flaring to life. Much too close for her comfort.

"I bet I called you something, too, during those nights. Your godmother said I had a special nickname for you, but she wouldn't tell me what it was." His gaze probed hers. "Are you planning on letting me in on the secret?"

"No." She dropped her arms to her sides and took a determined step back, grateful that she'd mustered the resources to make that last word firm. "Whatever you called me doesn't matter anymore, either."

He took another step forward, again bridging the gap between them, and she had no trouble seeing the challenge forming in his brilliantly blue eyes. "Do you mean to tell me that if I kissed you right this minute, you wouldn't feel anything?"

"You're not kissing me," she informed him in no uncertain terms.

And then he was.

Before she could get another word out, his mouth settled on hers. He didn't grab her, didn't tug her to him, didn't even put his hands on her. Just his mouth. And that was enough to have her standing stock-still as her pulse leaped.

Just as it always had.

That was when she began to feel, and all she could think as her eyes drifted shut was that it felt as though their lips had last touched yesterday. In a heartbeat, time hurled itself back to those nights when they'd never seemed to get enough of each other. Not when it came to kissing. Or what had followed.

His taste was undeniably familiar when she parted her lips in what had once been an inevitable response and took in a tangy mix of flavors, the essence of which was pure male. Pure Ryan Larabee. Except *pure* had nothing to do with it, as she'd known right from their very first dance on the evening they'd met, when he'd gazed down at her with an oh-so-sexy grin and called her something no one ever had before.

Something no one had called her for six long years, not since the day they'd stood on those courthouse steps, when he'd said goodbye and swore he would never forget her.

Abby sighed a soundless sigh. That dance had been the beginning of so many things. Some good. Some bad. *And some of which are better left alone,* a niggling voice in the back of her mind reminded her. *Don't let the memories take over. Don't let him make you remember too much, not about those nights, or you'll be sorry.*

But at the moment it seemed so far away. And he was so close. No matter what it told her, she couldn't heed that quiet voice of reason and bring things to a halt. Not now. Not yet. Not any more than she could stop a sudden shiver from racing up her spine.

Just as it always had.

Ryan felt it, the small tremble at the point where their mouths were joined, one that had come from the woman standing a bare inch away. It had him deepening the kiss even as his hands curled tight with his effort not to reach for her, not to fist his fingers in her flame-colored hair or cup his rough-skinned palm around her far-smoother chin. Instead he silently declared himself downright thankful that she wasn't stepping back, that she was participating in what he'd started, and concentrated on savoring what she now readily offered.

That, he was more than prepared to do.

She tasted…fresh, he decided, letting his tongue have its way. New. Nevertheless, a part of him recognized her from years earlier, as it had on his first day at Aunt Abigail's. Deep down, something inside him remembered, even if the rest of him could only imagine what they had shared in the past.

Luckily, he discovered he had a good imagination when it came to certain things. Vivid pictures were forming right now, ones involving soft skin and satin sheets. Yards of silky legs and the shortest of lacy nightgowns. And a bed the size of Texas, with plenty of room for a man to stretch out, and over. Yes, indeed. He didn't need total recall, not when he could—

"Ahem." The sound of a deep voice doing a not-too-delicate job of clearing a throat brought a rapid end to Ryan's reflections. And the kiss.

Hell.

He opened his eyes just as Abby pulled back with a hard blink. She glanced over his shoulder to where the sound had come from, then switched her gaze back to his in a flash. Even in the murky light he had no trouble seeing a steely glare forming, one she aimed straight at him.

"You are *not* kissing me again," she said through clenched teeth, her voice just loud enough to reach him. And then she slipped past him and wasted no time in leaving, not if the sharp creak of a door being yanked opened and swiftly shut was any indication.

Ryan inhaled a steadying drag of air, let it out and slowly switched around to find another steely gaze trained on him. This one belonged to someone who stood near the door Abby had just used, someone who looked in no mood to mince words.

"She's an engaged woman, you know," Bill Stockton said, crossing his arms over his chest.

"Trust me," Ryan muttered, "I'm well aware of that." Although he hadn't given it a thought when he'd launched that kiss, he had to admit.

"She didn't seem too happy with you when she made tracks out of here."

Ryan lifted a shoulder in a shrug. "Yeah, well, I'm not all that happy at the moment myself."

The older man studied him for a silent second. "You're stirred up, that's what you are," he said. "Hormones."

Right on, Ryan thought. His were still raging. "Thank you for your diagnosis," he said dryly. "You and Dr. Wonderful must have hit it off."

Bill snorted. "Doesn't take a doc to figure out what's wrong with you. And, just for the record, his name's Allan Drake."

"Humph."

"I don't think he's right for my wife's goddaughter any more than she does, if that's any consolation."

Ryan's mouth twisted. "Since I seem to be out of the picture, the whole thing shouldn't make any difference to me one way or the other." But it did, because he still wanted her—even more after that kiss.

Bill ambled forward to stand by the window. "Why don't you come over to my place on Monday?" he suggested in a friendlier tone. "The drive's easy on the eyes, since it's up toward the mountains, and I'll show you around. We can always flip a few burgers for lunch."

It was Ryan's turn to study the other man. "Feeling sorry for me, Stockton?" he asked.

"No." Bill smiled a wily smile. "I just figure smelling something besides sugar and spice might clear your head."

"And what am I going to smell at your place?"

"Horse manure."

Ryan ran his tongue around his teeth, thinking of what his sister had told him. "I'm fairly sure I got more than a whiff of that back when I was a kid."

"Good. We'll let you shovel some. Maybe it'll help jog your memory."

Ryan had to grin, despite everything. "Maybe it will."

"I'll bet the good doctor wouldn't be worth a lick at shoveling crap," Bill said.

"There is that," Ryan agreed. "Still, I'd just as soon you didn't mention the word *doctor* again. I've had my fill of them."

Bill nodded thoughtfully. "Too bad the woman who just huffed out of here hasn't."

"Yeah." Ryan turned and stared out at the moonlit night. "Too damn bad."

Chapter Four

"I've missed you, too, Allan," Abby told her fiancé over the phone on Monday morning.

"Too bad that with the seminar I have to attend I won't be able to make it to Harmony until the weekend after next," he replied, his deep voice as pleasing to the ear as always.

"Mmm-hmm," Abby agreed. But what was really too bad, she confessed to herself, was that she hadn't missed him all that much. Another man had been taking up far too many of her thoughts, which had been the case even before he'd started something on the back porch he'd had no business starting. And now it was even more of a challenge to block him from her mind.

Luckily, Sundays were usually busy at Aunt Abigail's. She'd managed to go for hours without thinking of Ryan at all yesterday, and had done a good job of avoiding him, as well. Today, of course, would be another matter. But if she couldn't completely avoid the man in question, she could—and would, she vowed—do her best to ignore him as much as possible and only be as civil as she had to be whenever they came in contact.

"Things have been hectic here," Allan said. "Spring colds have been making the rounds. It's a good thing I have Grace. I don't know how I'd get along without her."

Abby knew that Grace Carmichael had been with Allan since he'd opened his practice. Besides being a top-notch nurse, Grace had a talent for organization, and Allan had sung her praises on more than one occasion. "I hope you won't have to get along without her anytime soon," Abby said.

"I, ah, don't know about that."

"What do you mean?" Judging by his suddenly sober tone, something was worrying Allan. Abby could almost see a frown knitting his brow as he sat behind his desk, a handsome piece of traditional office furniture as solid and steady as its owner.

"I'm not sure what I mean," Allan admitted. "It's just that lately Grace has been acting a bit...strange."

Abby frowned her own frown at that news. "In what way?"

"Nothing definite that I can put a finger on." He released a long breath. "When it comes to dealing with the children and their parents, she's as soothingly cheerful as always. But whenever we're alone, she's coolly courteous, and that's about it. She used to do a lot of little extras for me without my asking. I never realized how many, actually, until she stopped altogether. Now I'm lucky if she says good morning when I walk in. Sometimes I get no more than a brisk nod and a I-have-better-things-to-do-than-be-sociable-to-you look."

"Mmm." Abby was beginning to get a glimmer. "When did you first notice the change?"

Allan mulled that over for a second. "It started

around the time I returned from your godmother's wedding, now that I think about it.''

Shortly after she and Allan became engaged, Abby thought. The timing fit the theory forming in her mind too well to disregard. But what could she tell him? *Your nurse has a thing for you, and she's not exactly thrilled that you're marrying someone else.*

And if she did say as much, would Allan really believe it? Most likely not, Abby decided, more than suspecting that he viewed Grace Carmichael as a skilled caregiver, valuable employee and casual friend, period. It would probably never occur to him that Grace, who was single and only a few years older than her boss, might be interested in him on a man-and-woman level.

Not that Grace went out of her way to make the male half of the population see her in that light, Abby had to concede. Whenever she herself had visited the office with Cara, Grace's hair, which was every bit as strikingly gold as Allan's, had been scraped back in a tight bun, a coat of clear lip gloss her only concession to makeup. Still, her wire-rimmed glasses had rested on a delicately upturned nose, and the rest of her features might well have shone with a few enhancements. What needed no enhancing was her full figure. Minus the crisply pressed uniform it regularly hid behind, Abby had little doubt of its potential to turn many male heads.

''She's leaving early today, too,'' Allan grumbled, breaking into Abby's reflections. ''Grace used to stay late to catch up on things, but not anymore. She didn't even ask if it was convenient for her to take the afternoon off. She just flat-out told me she was out of here at three o'clock, and not because of any sort of emergency, either. Something about a shoe sale at the mall, for Pete's sake.''

Abby had to smile, thinking that even if her fiancé was raking a frustrated hand through his expertly cut hair, as she imagined might well be the case, it would effortlessly fall into place. Allan always looked as if he'd just stepped from the pages of a medical journal, the calmly composed professional in every respect.

One thing for certain, he was nothing like Ryan Larabee.

Abby leaned back in her armchair and glanced around the simply furnished bedroom she'd been occupying since her arrival in Harmony, realizing she had to tell Allan about Ryan's sudden reappearance in her life. But first she had to put a diplomatic end to the subject of Grace's behavior without revealing her suspicions. Even assuming they were correct, she had no plans to help Allan solve the puzzle. If Grace had a secret yen for him, she was entitled to keep it private.

Abby knew the value of a woman's pride.

"This whole matter with Grace may eventually work out," she said, summoning a reassuring tone.

"God, I hope so," he replied. "I just want things to go back to the way they were."

Maybe they never would, Abby thought. But who knew? "While we're on the subject of recent events," she said, "I have something to tell you." And with that Abby went on to explain, as briefly as possible, what had happened since she'd met a man from her past on the bed and breakfast's doorstep. She did her best to keep emotions out of it, and not for the world would she mention that kiss. "So he intends to stay for a while," she summed up minutes later, "and he may well be here next weekend during your visit."

Allan took a moment to digest that information. "I didn't think I'd ever meet the man you were once married to, but I can't say the prospect bothers me. After all, your relationship ended a long time ago."

Yes, but he can still make me feel too much, Abby silently acknowledged, resisting the urge to sigh long and hard. Hopefully Allan's visit would be just what she needed to put things in perspective. There was no point in rehashing the memories, of that much she was sure. Ryan Larabee and whatever she'd once felt for him belonged to the past.

Another man was her—and Cara's—future.

ABBY MADE HER WAY downstairs soon after winding up her conversation with Allan. The house was quiet. Most of the guests had left the day before. Only Ryan and Major Hobbs, a retired army man from Virginia, remained. She'd noticed them eating breakfast together in the dining room earlier but hadn't lingered after feeding Cara in the kitchen, preferring to keep out of Ryan's way.

So far no words had passed between them since Saturday evening. She'd be happy if they never spoke again, all things considered, but the more practical parts of her didn't hold out much hope for that. No, her best bet was to go about her own business and have as little to do with him as possible.

With that goal firmly in mind, Abby entered the kitchen and was grateful to find only Ethel and Cara there. Both wore yellow today—one a daisy-print apron, the other a stretchy cotton romper. Ethel was seated at the table, thumbing through the local newspaper, while Cara sat in her portable playpen, thumping a wooden spoon on an empty cereal box.

"She keeps the beat pretty well," Ethel remarked to Abby. "We may have a rock-and-roll drummer in the making."

"Thanks for keeping an eye on her," Abby said. "I needed some quiet time to talk to Allan."

Ethel lifted an eyebrow. "I know it's not any of my affair, but I can't help wondering if you told him about Ryan."

Abby's short nod answered the question. "Even if I'd wanted to avoid the issue," she said, "I didn't have much choice. Unless Ryan changes his mind about staying, he'll be here when Allan drives up next weekend."

"The good doctor is paying us a visit?" a deep voice asked from the doorway.

Releasing a resigned breath, Abby turned around. "Yes."

Ryan leaned against the doorjamb and crossed his arms over the front of his denim shirt. "Can't wait to meet him."

"I don't think he precisely shares your enthusiasm," she replied, "but he'll be here regardless."

His tone still as dry as dust, Ryan said, "What a guy." Straightening, he ambled into the room, his boots scraping softly on the tile. "Mind telling me exactly what he looks like?"

"He's about as tall as you are," Ethel replied politely when Abby remained silent. "Blond hair and an unusual shade of eyes. What would you say the color was, dear?" she asked Abby, who kept her gaze on Ryan.

"Lavender."

"Lavender?" Ryan did nothing to hide a very male grimace. "Isn't that one of the fancy soaps you keep in the bathrooms here? I almost used it in the shower before I realized how I'd wind up smelling."

Abby lifted her chin. "For your information, Allan's eyes are one of his best features."

"If you say so."

"I most certainly do."

That said, Abby walked over to the cabinets, picked up a mug and poured herself some coffee, deciding she could always dump it over Ryan's far-too-attractive head if he got too irritating. He was still a guest, though, so she'd probably resist temptation. Maybe.

"I could use another dose of caffeine myself," Ryan said as he joined her at the counter. He fixed his coffee, then lifted the mug to his mouth and studied her over the rim as he downed a long swallow. "Wish I could remember if you made coffee as great as Ethel's."

He'd dropped his voice a notch with that last comment. Not that it was strictly necessary to keep their conversation private, Abby knew. Ethel had gone back to the newspaper and Cara was still pounding away. "I was never anywhere near as good as Ethel in the kitchen," she admitted.

"Too bad for the doc."

Abby shrugged. "Allan thinks about more than his stomach."

He smiled a meaningful smile. "I didn't say food was everything."

"For the record, you were hardly a wonder in the kitchen yourself," she told him, not mincing words.

"Hmm." Ryan leaned against the counter. "How is the doctor in that department?"

Abby took a short sip of her coffee and opted for the truth. "Actually, I don't know."

"You do all the cooking?"

"We go out to dinner."

He hesitated a bare second. "How about breakfast?"

She set her mug down on the counter with an audible snap. "I believe that's none of your business."

His gaze sharpened, though he kept his voice mild. "I'm getting the feeling you haven't shared many breakfasts. Or any. Not yet." Again his smile surfaced and grew. "Well, well. Your fiancé seems to be a slow worker."

"Not that I should be dignifying that remark with a reply," Abby huffed out, goaded into responding, "but we *both* decided to take things at a slower pace."

Neither of them had declared their undying love, either, she reflected. It was too soon. She more than suspected that Allan would never have proposed marriage when he had if she hadn't mentioned the very real possibility of her moving to Harmony to manage Aunt Abigail's. He wasn't the impulsive type. Even on somewhat short acquaintance, given that they'd known each other only a matter of months, she was positive of that. And, although it hadn't always been the case, heaven knows, she had learned the wisdom of looking before leaping.

"The rest will come in time," she added firmly.

"Including an engagement ring?" Ryan asked with a brief glance at the bare fingers of her left hand.

"As it happens, Allan will be bringing it with

him,'' she said. "The ring has been in his family for some time. He's having it resized for me.''

"What a guy,'' Ryan said one more time before he finished his coffee in a single gulp, looking far too pleased with what he'd discovered about her and Allan's relationship. Stepping away, he placed his mug in the sink and raised his voice a notch. "I'll leave you ladies to the rest of your morning. I'm going out, but I'll be back later this afternoon.''

"We're having pork chops for dinner,'' Ethel informed him, glancing up from her paper.

"Sounds great.'' He turned toward the hall door. "Bye.''

"Ba-ba,'' Cara said, halting in midbeat. She tossed the spoon down and lifted a tiny hand.

Ethel smiled. "Isn't that sweet? The little darling's waving bye-bye.''

Ryan aimed a look over his shoulder just in time to get the full effect of Cara's next statement as she fixed him with a steady stare. "Poop!''

"Oh, my,'' Ethel murmured after a stark second of silence. "Does she mean...?''

Abby barely held back a laugh as Ryan walked out a moment later, muttering something under his breath. "She certainly does,'' she cheerfully told the older woman. She walked over to the playpen and lifted Cara out for a hearty hug. "Good girl,'' she whispered in the baby's tiny ear.

Cara giggled and clapped her hands, looking thoroughly satisfied with herself.

RYAN WAS SMILING again as he negotiated a bend in the road leading up to the Stockton place, the sleek silver sports car he drove responding readily to his commands. So the former Mrs. Larabee and Dr. Wonderful hadn't made it as far as the bedroom, he thought. Why did that make him feel so damn good? Which he did, no question about it. He felt better than he had in days.

One thing for sure, even minus his memory he was dead certain that Abby's current engagement was no repeat of her first one, not by a long shot. No one had taken it slow then. If he'd had any doubts on that score, the kiss he hadn't been able to resist would have put a swift end to them. Not to mention the way she'd shivered in his arms.

Slow? Uh-uh. More like fast and furious. Yes, indeed. That he could believe.

Ryan sat back to enjoy what remained of the drive and soon learned that the Stockton place was a long way from new. As ranches went, it was probably smaller than average, consisting mainly of a sprawling white frame house, an old barn painted brick-red, and a few corrals scattered around the area. The view, on the other hand, was impressive enough to have most anyone's eyes widening, and Ryan was no exception.

With a low, pine-studded mountain providing a backdrop and the city spread out below, the scene was worthy of a picture postcard. Accepting the invitation to visit had been a good move, Ryan decided as he started up a gravel driveway leading to the house. It would have been a shame to miss this.

Bill came out to greet his visitor, letting the weathered screen door slap shut behind him. Again he wore Wranglers and a checked shirt, today with a wide-brimmed brown hat.

Ryan got out of the car, reached in for his black

Stetson and tapped it down on his head low enough to shade his eyes from the midday sun. "Nice spot," he said as his host approached.

"Glad you think so," Bill replied. "I've got instructions from my wife to tell you she was sorry she couldn't be here. She had a committee meeting. There's a dance being held to tie in with Harmony's annual spring rodeo in a few weeks and it takes some planning to put it on, what with the number of folks expected to attend."

One particular word among the rest caught Ryan's attention. "A rodeo?"

Bill dipped his head in a nod. "Been going on every spring for ages. Calf roping, steer wrestling, bull riding. Draws a lot of people, both to watch and compete. A person can make a decent living on the rodeo tour if they're good at it. I did it for years when I was younger."

"I did a little of it, too," Ryan said, remembering a recent phone conversation. "My sister, who now owns the family ranch in Wyoming, just told me the other day that one of the things I did to scrape up money for flying lessons was enter local rodeo competitions."

"You don't say." Bill studied his guest for a moment. "Any particular event?"

"Bull riding."

The older man threw back his head and laughed out loud. "Well, if that don't beat all. It was my preference, too. Nothing like the feel of one-ton-plus of prime beef bucking under you. Wild Bill Stockton, they used to call me. Hardly original, I suppose, but I've got to admit I did my best to live up to the title at one time. I traveled all over the country and rode more bulls than you can shake a stick at before I packed it in and bought a small spread in Colorado. I'd probably still be there if I hadn't run into an old friend from my early days in Harmony. He mentioned that my high-school sweetheart had lost her husband a few years earlier.''

''So you came back,'' Ryan summed up.

''You bet, and didn't waste any time about it, either. I lost her the first time around because I was set on seeing some of the world and her folks convinced her that sharing a life with me on the road wasn't what was best for her. Maybe they were right, too, at least in some ways. I can see that now. Anyway, I wound up buying this place and dropping on one bony knee to ask her to marry me.''

The corners of Ryan's mouth slid up as an image formed in his mind of this formidable man down on his knees before an equally formidable woman. ''I guess that worked, huh?''

Bill smiled a wily smile. ''I was prepared to toss her over my shoulder and haul her to the altar, but she decided to take it easy on me.'' He switched around and started toward the barn. ''Come on, I'll give you a tour before we head back to the house for lunch. There's somebody I want you to meet.''

Who could that be? Ryan wondered as he fell into step beside Bill and slid his hands into his pockets. Their boots crunched on packed gravel as they made their way toward the rear of the property, a mild breeze drifting down from the mountains ruffling their clothing. ''What do you plan on doing with this place?'' Ryan asked, noting that at the moment there wasn't much activity going on.

''After I get it in shape, I'll bring in some horses

for training. That's what I've been doing for the last several years. There's a profitable market for a well-trained animal.''

They entered the large barn, most of which was divided into stalls of various sizes. Two full-grown horses occupied front slots. Both shook their heads and whinnied a soft greeting, sending their long manes swaying.

''Custer and Pinto have been with me for a while,'' Bill explained as he headed toward the rear of the barn. ''They've become good friends of mine, just like the guy in the back. He's the one I want you to meet.''

A visitor like himself? Ryan thought. Or a ranch hand, maybe? The title *friend* could cover a lot of ground. Heck, it might even be a dog.

It turned out to be a bull.

And not just any bull, Ryan saw with one sweeping glance. A big bull. Rust-colored, with a white face and short horns, the animal was downright massive.

''This is Lively,'' Bill said by way of introduction. ''He spent his fair share of time in rodeo arenas in his younger days, just like I did. By the time I bought him, some people figured he was past his prime, but they were wrong. I'm thinking about letting him show the folks in Harmony a thing or two at the rodeo coming up. Lively's still got some good years left in him.''

Ryan had his doubts. The bull, as large as it was, had barely moved since they'd approached the stall, merely blinking its dark eyes as it viewed the men standing with their forearms braced on the top slat. ''I guess I'll have to take your word for it,'' he said, mustering a neutral tone.

Bill slid him a look. "I'd give you a demonstration just to prove my point, but unfortunately my bones can't take too much rattling anymore."

But my bones can. Ryan stilled as that thought struck. He'd ridden bulls in the past. Why couldn't he now? *Because you're still recovering from the accident,* a niggling voice reminded him. He found himself in no mood to listen. And besides, he'd been doing his exercises. His leg hadn't even bothered him lately, and the rest of him felt as good as new.

"Maybe I could give it a try," he said.

A probing glint snapped to life in Bill's gaze. "You remember how?"

"Not exactly," Ryan admitted. "But I was apparently good enough at it to earn some money in the past, and I'd be willing to bet the mechanics will come back to me once the action starts." *Plus this bull doesn't look like he'd provide all that much action anyway,* he added to himself.

"All right," Bill agreed after studying his guest for another moment. "Lively could use the exercise, and I'm glad to have somebody oblige him. Just so you know, you don't have to worry about scrambling out of his way once the ride's over. He won't try to stomp on you like another bull might. He's got his own way of putting a cap on things."

"What's that?"

Bill's wily smile reappeared. "You'll find out, if you still want to give it a try."

Ryan nodded and tapped his hat down another notch. "Let's do it."

Bill pulled the stall door open with a creaking sound. "Come on, Lively. You've got a customer."

The huge animal ambled out, head hanging, and

followed its owner past a wide doorway at the far end of the barn and into an adjoining corral. Ryan brought up the rear, shaking his head and thinking that Lively seemed to be anything but. This had to be the tamest bull in creation, or maybe just the laziest.

Bill slipped two long leather straps around the bull's muscled torso. One strap threaded with a thick length of rope went behind its front legs. The other strap was positioned farther down its body, with a short portion of the front rope left free to drop down the animal's side.

"Some greenhorns think we bind a bull's privates to make him kick higher." Bill snorted. "Any male with common sense would realize that wouldn't work worth a damn if he thought about it. I mean, how high would a man kick if somebody strapped up his privates? He'd probably drop flat to the ground and moan like a mangy dog."

Ryan held back a wince. "You've got a point."

Bill straightened and led Lively to a narrow wooden chute built at one side of the corral. "Okay," he told Ryan, "you climb on up the side, throw your legs over the top and ease yourself down on Lively's back, then lock one hand around the front strap. Just to jog your memory, in a competition the rules say you have to stay on at least eight seconds to be judged. Anything less doesn't count."

Ryan nodded, thinking he could surely stay on that long, and did as instructed. The bull didn't move a muscle as he perched himself on its back and fisted his hand around the strap.

"Ready?" Bill asked.

"Yeah."

Bill stepped back. "Time, Lively!"

Lively moved at last—and swiftly—charging out of the chute. Before Ryan knew it they were in the middle of the corral and the world was whirling around him as the bull did a fast spin. After that the bucking started while Ryan held on tight, automatically leaning forward for a better-balanced position as instinct kicked in. His free arm, held high now, rocked back and forth. His heart pounded in his chest. His whole body tightened with the effort to stay on.

And then he was airborne.

He landed on his butt, the breath knocked out of him. After drawing in a long drag of air, then another, he slowly got to his knees, glanced up and found himself being studied by the bull, its unblinking dark eyes inches away. Finally, it lifted its broad nose, as if to express pure bovine disgust, then turned and ambled back to the barn.

Ryan rose to his feet just as Bill's low chuckle reached him. He looked over at the side of the corral. "Okay, so now I know how the program ends."

"Always gets a big hand from the crowd," Bill cheerfully informed him. "You've got to go the full eight seconds to win Lively's approval."

Ryan grimaced. "What does he do, time his riders?"

Bill shrugged. "Could be he has an internal stopwatch. I had to rely on the one in my pocket." He lifted a hand and held it up for Ryan's inspection.

"How long did I last?" Ryan asked.

"Just under five seconds."

"*Five* seconds." He couldn't believe it. A short lifetime had seemed to pass before he'd gone sailing through the air.

"Look on the bright side," Bill told him. "You

didn't break anything, most especially your neck. My wife wouldn't have been too happy with me if that had happened, not to mention the women over at Aunt Abigail's.''

Ryan rubbed his backside as he walked to where the older man stood. ''One particular woman over there might not have minded all that much.''

Bill cocked an eyebrow. ''You kiss her again?''

''No.''

''Still want to?''

Ryan didn't have to think about it. He knew the answer full well. ''Yeah,'' he said.

His host nodded. ''Well, I guess your hormones survived the ride, too. Let's have lunch.''

A THICK HAMBURGER served with a side of smoky cowboy beans went a long way toward restoring Ryan's good mood. He leaned back in one of the wrought-iron chairs set under a shade tree in the Stocktons' backyard and patted his flat stomach.

''You grill a good burger,'' he told the man seated across the table from him.

''Thanks,'' Bill replied. ''It's always been a mystery to me how I can manage to burn half of what I try to make on the stove when I don't seem to have much trouble dealing with a heap of hot charcoal.''

''For what it's worth, you're not alone. My former wife didn't hesitate to tell me I was a dud in the kitchen during the time we were married,'' Ryan confessed with a wry twist of his lips.

Bill propped his elbows on the table and fixed his guest with a shrewd gaze. ''I doubt that's why you got divorced, though.''

''No.''

"Want to talk about it?"

Ryan stretched his long legs out and stacked one booted foot over the other. "Not especially."

"Okay," Bill said. "I'll admit I'm as ready as the next male to steer clear of the sort of relationship—excuse the word," he slid in dryly "—chats females seem to favor, so I'll just pass along one piece of what I consider wisdom before I shut my jaws on the matter." He paused, then spaced out his next words. "I've learned—mainly the hard way, I can't deny—that a man has to decide what's most important to him and keep his priorities straight. End of subject."

"Good advice, I guess," Ryan murmured after a moment, wondering if his father had ever sat him down and advised him on how to go on in life. He wished he knew. He hadn't followed in his father's footsteps, that was certain. It occurred to him that he might well never have set foot on a ranch after leaving the family homestead for good. Until today.

"Your bones still rattling?" Bill asked mildly, keeping his word and switching subjects.

Ryan blew out a breath. "Let's just say I still have a bone to pick with Lively."

Bill's gaze lit with clear amusement. "Does that mean you plan on riding him again?"

Ryan found himself answering with a question of his own. "Can anyone enter the rodeo that's coming up?"

Bill sat back, obviously surprised. "Well, I'll be... Do you mean it?"

Ryan discovered he did, thinking it would prove something, mainly to himself. His supervisors at the Border Patrol thought he was loony tunes. His career had gone down the tubes. His memory was still a blank wall in his mind.

But he didn't need his memory or his job to tackle this particular challenge. Sheer male pride was as much a factor as anything else, he supposed, but whatever the case, he couldn't turn down a chance to claim a small personal victory by staying on a bucking bull's back for at least eight seconds.

"Yes, I mean it," he said deliberately.

Bill stared at him. "I see you do," he replied at last. "And to answer your question, anybody's welcome to enter. You just need to register and pay the entry fee."

Ryan nodded. "I'm going to need some practice."

"Damn right," Bill didn't hesitate to tell him. "I imagine Lively will be glad to oblige you."

"Can we keep this private between the three of us?"

"You, me and the bull?" Bill mulled that over for a moment. "We don't get much company out here. Haven't yet, at any rate. I guess because folks still consider us newlyweds. You shouldn't have much problem practicing with Lively on a hush-hush basis. My wife's another story, though. She's going to have to know, but she'll keep it quiet if we ask her to."

"All right," Ryan agreed. "I appreciate your letting me do this. Thanks."

"None needed." Bill lifted his soda can and polished off his cola. "All I'm asking is that you try not to break your neck in the process. Take it easy, and do your best when the time comes. Remember, the rodeo is the last weekend in May."

The last weekend in May.

Suddenly those words echoed repeatedly in Ryan's

mind, capturing his thoughts. *The last weekend in May.* He sat straight up, his gaze widening with the knowledge of what had just happened.

A small part of his past had just resurfaced.

Chapter Five

"What's wrong?" Bill's expression had sobered in a heartbeat. "Are you okay, son?"

"Yeah." Ryan hoped to heaven it was true. His mind still reeled from the impact of the words tumbling through it. He raised a hand and rubbed his eyes, then dropped it and leaned back again, releasing a long breath.

"What in holy hell happened? I have to tell you that for a second there you looked like you saw a ghost."

"Actually," Ryan said slowly, "I saw…my past. I don't know how else to explain it. A memory hit me—" he snapped his fingers "—just like that. A comment you made started it."

Bill frowned. "About the rodeo?"

"No. It was your mentioning the last weekend in May. Something's going to happen then. Something important that has nothing to do with the rodeo. My gut is telling me that loud and clear right this minute." Ryan fisted his hand in frustration. "Trouble is, my brain can't figure out what it means. I got a glimpse of it, and then it was gone."

"Did you get a bad sense about this thing?"

The question was straightforward enough to assure Ryan that Bill was taking him seriously. "God, you don't think I'm crazy. I have to thank you again."

Bill dismissed that statement with a soft snort. "By the time a person has traveled as wide and seen as much as I have, he'd be a sorry case if he hadn't learned enough to keep an open mind. I've got no reason not to believe you, so I do. It's as simple as that."

A brief smile tugged at Ryan's lips. "I suppose it is. And no, I didn't exactly get a bad feeling. More of an urgent one is how I'd describe it. The only thing I'm dead certain of is that it's important for me to remember whatever it is."

"You just might," Bill said. "Could well be that if it popped into your head once, it will again. The trick may be not to dwell on it. I don't plan on saying anything to anyone, that's for sure. This is your business, as far as I'm concerned. And there's a ways to go before the end of May, after all."

"You're right," Ryan decided after thinking it over. "Either it comes to me or it doesn't. I'll nose around a bit, see if it might tie in with anything my acquaintances down south know about. Other than that, there's not much I can do."

"Sounds like the right approach," Bill agreed. "I figure a smart man knows when to bide his time. And you'll have plenty to keep you occupied. You've got your work cut out for you, you know, if you're going to take on Lively."

"Did I hear something about taking on that huge bull?" Gail Stockton asked as she approached from the house. She wore a navy shirtwaist dress, matching low-heeled pumps and a white blazer with the sleeves pushed up to the elbows. Reaching the men a moment later, she leaned over and gave her husband a quick kiss, then straightened and shook a small finger at him. "Don't even think about it, Wild Bill. Your bull-riding days are over."

"I'm not the bull rider in question, honeybun," he said, gazing up at her. "Our guest is the one with plans not only to ride Lively but to enter the Harmony rodeo to boot."

Gail's eyebrows shot up. "Why, for heaven's sake?" she asked, then sank into a chair and heard her companions out in silence as they explained the situation. "Okay," she said at last, "I'm not endorsing this idea, not by any means, but I'll agree to keep it private."

Bill looked at Ryan. "Told you she would."

Gail leaned back and folded her arms under her breasts. "Now I have something to tell you both," she said. "I stopped by to see Abby and Ethel on my way back from the committee meeting. While I was there, Ethel got a phone call from her daughter in California, and it wasn't cheerful news."

Frowning, Bill asked, "What's the deal?"

"I think I mentioned to you that Ethel's seventieth birthday is this Friday, and that her daughter and son-in-law planned to fly into Phoenix and drive up to spend the day with her." Gail sighed. "Unfortunately, her son-in-law had to have an emergency appendectomy last night. He'll be fine, and Ethel was certainly happy to learn that he's in no danger, but the fact remains that even though they're going to reschedule their visit after he recuperates, none of Ethel's family will be here for her birthday. And seventy is a milestone."

"Hope I make it," Bill drawled.

"You will," his wife assured him. "I intend to make sure you take good care of yourself." She sat forward. "Now, about Ethel. After the phone call, Abby and I put our heads together and decided to throw a party on Friday evening at Aunt Abigail's. And not just any party."

She paused, glancing from one man to the other. "I'm asking you both to help with this, because I want it to be one of the nicest—if not the biggest— parties this town has ever seen. Although Ethel would never say so, being the upbeat kind of person she is, celebrating this particular birthday without her only child here to be part of it had to be a major disappointment. I'd like to try to make it up to her."

"Ethel's okay in my book, even if she is a card-sharp," Ryan said, lifting his soda can for a final swallow. "I don't know what I can do, but count me in."

"Ditto," Bill offered in agreement.

"Good." Gail looked at Ryan. "You and Abby will be in charge of the food."

Ryan nearly choked on his cola. "The *food?*" he finally got out. "Didn't my ex-wife tell you I'm hopeless in that area?"

"No," Gail said. "Maybe," she added casually, "because I forgot to mention I planned to ask you to help her."

"Uh-huh." Ryan narrowed his gaze. "Why *did* you ask me?"

Gail lifted one delicate shoulder in a shrug. "Bill and I know a lot more people in Harmony than you and Abby do, so it only makes sense for us to take charge of notifying Ethel's friends and making sure they'll be there to shout 'Surprise!' at the appropriate moment. We can also get Ethel out of the house on some pretext so you and Abby will be able to set things up on Friday.''

''Uh-huh,'' Ryan repeated. ''And the former Mrs. Larabee will be overjoyed to find herself saddled with my help.'' His tone was riddled with irony.

''It will all work out,'' Gail said confidently. Her smile was wide. ''This is going to be a surprise party to remember.''

''That,'' Ryan muttered, ''is what I'm afraid of.''

He was also afraid, and more than a little, that he might not remember what his gut told him he needed to. Not in time, at any rate. *What in blazes was scheduled to happen the last weekend in May?*

Ryan wished to hell he knew.

ABBY PLANTED her fists on her hips. It was either that or throw her hands up in exasperation. ''As I've already said more than once, we have to make this party special, and serving snacks alone, even mounds of them, isn't going to cut it.''

''Why not?'' Ryan asked as he lounged in one of the back-porch wicker chairs. ''Chips, dips, pretzels and popcorn—all four of the major food groups, you could say. Add some soda and beer to drink, and I don't see any reason that wouldn't fit the bill.''

''Spoken like a true uninformed male.''

Ryan cocked an eyebrow. ''I thought I was the expert on how to throw parties?''

''Not this kind,'' Abby countered without hesitation, frowning down at him. ''We at least have to serve some small finger sandwiches, maybe with some cut-up vegetables and cheese and crackers. Plus we need a bowl of punch," she added after a moment's consideration.

"Punch?" Ryan made a face. "You mean that fruity sweet stuff?"

"Some people happen to like it," Abby pointed out.

"Well, I'm not one of them."

"How can you be so sure of that if you can't remember?" she asked dryly.

"Instinct," he told her, crossing his arms over the front of his shirt.

Abby's own instincts urged her to stomp a foot on his booted toes. If she'd been wearing high heels, the temptation might have been irresistible. The leather loafers she wore wouldn't make nearly as much of an impact. Which was really too bad.

In the thirty minutes since this discussion had started, she and Ryan had only managed to agree on ordering a birthday cake from one of the local bakeries. Had he been this contrary when they were married? No, more on the easygoing side was how she recalled him. Basically, he'd been happy if he could fly most days and party half the night away on a regular basis. Back then, he hadn't been a complicated man.

Now that seemed to have changed, enough in any case to have her wondering what was going on inside him. Unless she was mistaken, and despite his currently laid-back posture as he calmly viewed her with an even expression, something was troubling him. Something that went beyond his understandable frustration about the accident and its consequences. Whether she was reading him correctly or not, though, there was no question that he was trying her patience at the moment. Maybe not intentionally, but the end result was the same.

"We're serving punch," she said with firm determination. "I'll make it, and you can deal with the soda and beer."

He shrugged and nodded his agreement. "I hope you put something in the stuff to at least kick it up a notch."

"I don't think that will be necessary," Abby replied. She kept her tone mild with some effort, then looked away from him as the third person in the room suddenly made a bid for her attention.

"Ma!" Cara said. Standing with a tight grip on one side of her mesh playpen, she held her favorite toy, a stuffed horse, in her free hand and smacked her rosy lips.

"Guess you're ready for your midmorning juice," Abby concluded with a fond smile, always mindful of the importance of food in this particular child's life. "I'll get it ready and be right back."

And with that she left Ryan alone for the first time with a tiny person who hadn't hesitated in the past to aim a zinger his way. Deciding to head it off this time, he got up, walked over and slowly hunkered down beside the playpen.

"Don't even think about it," he said softly yet firmly, looking straight into a pair of dark eyes that slanted up at the sides. "I'm nobody's granddaddy, so just get that out of your head right now."

Cara met him stare for stare for a long moment, then glanced down at the toy horse, peeked up again at Ryan, and finally smiled an oh-so-innocent smile just before she said, "Poop!"

Ryan sat back on his denim-clad haunches. "You," he told her flat-out, "are a little devil."

That statement only earned him a merry giggle as the baby plopped down on the seat of a blue terry cloth outfit decorated with tiny clouds and chubby angels.

"Don't think I'm giving up that easily," he said. "If I can take on a huge bull, I should be able to convince a pint-size person to see things my way." Eventually, he added to himself, figuring he had his work cut out for him here, too. "You may be every bit as stubborn as your mother," he went on, "but I'll let you in on a secret. I'm not just rolling over and letting her totally have her way about Ethel's big day, whatever she might believe."

Her dusky curls held back by a frilly white band, Cara tilted her head to one side, as if to ask what he meant.

Ryan was glad to oblige her. "For a start," he explained, leaning in and dropping his voice, "I'm putting a little something extra in the punch to zip it up. And then..." He paused, seeking another idea. It didn't take him long to come up with one. "And then," he continued, "considering Ethel's taste in music, I think she'd probably appreciate a visit from a hip-grinding, raspy-voiced rock star. Or as close to one as I can find between now and Friday."

After all, Ryan thought as the baby went back to playing with her toy, he seemed to have a party-throwing reputation to maintain. Maybe it wasn't the most admirable of traits, but he still didn't plan on taking it lightly.

RYAN RAN UP a substantial phone bill during the next few days, calling everyone he considered a possible source of information about the small part of his past that had resurfaced out of nowhere. It was no easy task, he found out as he made one contact after another, sometimes acting on a suggestion that would lead him to talk to yet another person. Call after call, he kept his questions as casual as he could under the circumstances and his disappointment to himself when the individual he spoke to could not think of anything out of the ordinary that was scheduled to happen the last weekend in May.

Nothing.

By Friday morning he'd nearly resigned himself to giving the whole thing up as a lost cause when Ethel phoned from one of the kitchen lines in the middle of his exercise routine to tell him she was transferring a call upstairs. It turned out to be from one of the first people he'd called earlier that week, Mac Dempsey.

Mac, a rugged Irishman close to Ryan's age, had visited Ryan in the hospital and shaken his head in sympathy over the memory loss without making a production of it. As Mac had explained then, he might well have been the last Border Patrol agent working outside of Ryan's own particular unit to see him before the accident.

"I got to thinking more about what you asked me a few days ago," Mac told Ryan in a deep, rumbling baritone. "I'm afraid I still can't come up with any ideas about the end of May, but I'm beginning to wonder if it just might be connected in some way with the Sonora Lounge."

Ryan sat on the edge of his bed, receiver in hand. "The place where you said we bumped into each other on the night before I crashed?"

"Uh-huh. It's a nice spot. Not fancy, but not a dive, either, like some of the bars in the border area, and you can get a decent meal there, too." Mac paused for a beat. "We only talked for a minute that evening. I was set to go in when you walked out. Looking back, though, I have to say that you seemed…preoccupied. I suppose that would be the best word to describe it. Unless I miss my guess, you were mulling something over—and fairly hard, to boot."

Ryan frowned thoughtfully. "Too bad I don't have a clue at the moment as to what that might have been."

"Sorry I can't be more specific," Mac said.

Unwilling to drop the subject while a chance remained to learn more, Ryan asked, "I was alone when I left the lounge?"

"Yeah."

"And when you went in, did you see anyone familiar?"

"Can't say I did," the other man replied after a brief hesitation. "It was late by that time, and the place wasn't busy. As far as I can recall, there were a couple of guys at the bar and a few people seated at some of the side tables. Anyway," he added, "I decided to pass along what I could about that night for what it's worth."

"Thanks, I appreciate it," Ryan said, and he did.

When the conversation ended, Ryan hung up the phone, closed his eyes and taxed his brain to come up with some indication of whether what he'd just learned was significant. No dice, he was forced to concede at last. The blank wall in his mind wasn't giving an inch.

Dammit.

Ryan raked a hand through his hair, well aware that he'd just wind up spinning his wheels if he tried to push it. Experience had taught him how useless that approach could be. Instead, deciding to forgo the rest of his exercises, he got up and headed for a shave and shower. He knew he had a busy day ahead of him, including a practice session with a bull. It would be the first since he'd become acquainted with Lively, and he was bound to get some exercise of a different kind—without breaking anything, he hoped.

And, after his visit to the Stockton ranch, he'd volunteered to go grocery shopping and pick up Ethel's birthday cake. Abby had already issued instructions to make sure not to return until Ethel was safely out of the house. Ryan shook his head. As if he couldn't come to that conclusion on his own.

Then again, while he couldn't deny that the former Mrs. Larabee's recent take-charge attitude had become a small thorn in his side, he definitely had something to look forward to. Ethel wasn't the only one, he reminded himself, with a surprise in store for her this evening.

It was simple justice, Ryan thought as he viewed his image in the bathroom mirror and stroked a palm over his beard-roughened jaw. He'd been thrown for a loop on more than one occasion by the things he'd discovered since arriving in Harmony. He figured it was someone else's turn.

ABBY BEGAN to get a glimmer of the fact that things weren't going to go entirely as she'd planned when Ryan arrived back at Aunt Abigail's midafternoon on

Friday sporting an odd little smile and looking thoroughly pleased with himself.

It was true that, per her reminder, he had waited to return until after Gail and Bill had taken Ethel on a shopping trip to Harmony's downtown, one scheduled to be followed by a visit to the local ice-cream parlor for hot fudge sundaes all around. A new outfit of Ethel's choosing would be their birthday gift, the Stocktons had explained, and Ethel had gone along with that idea without much protest. They'd also taken Cara with them, ostensibly to give Abby a short break from her maternal duties, but really to allow her enough free time to get everything in place for their return and the big surprise.

It was true, too, that Ryan had returned with all of the items on the grocery list she'd given him and had picked up the cake, as well. No, she couldn't fault him on that score. Neither could she deny that it had been thoughtful of him to volunteer for the assignment in the first place.

What she hadn't counted on, however, were the "extras" he'd decided to buy on his own, starting with a seemingly endless supply of snacks—chips, dips, pretzels and popcorn—and ending with a Mexican piñata filled with hard candy ready to spill out once someone, presumably the "birthday girl," broke it open.

The piñata was shaped like a donkey, and the donkey was covered with sequins. Small, glittering, glued-on sequins in every shade of the rainbow.

The donkey was also by no stretch of the imagination small.

Good Lord, Abby thought, studying the object. Made of thick layered paper, it had sharp, pointy ears, a short, fat tail, and was tall enough standing with its tube-shaped legs planted on the kitchen counter to look her straight in the eye. "Don't you think Ethel is a little, ah, mature for this kind of thing?" she asked.

Ryan raised a shoulder in a shrug and kept emptying grocery bags. "I figure she may still be game to take a whack at it."

"It doesn't exactly go with the rest of the decorations," Abby pointed out as diplomatically as possible, well aware that was a gross understatement. She and her godmother had opted for a green-and-white outdoor theme, one that featured ivy-patterned disposable tablecloths, plates and napkins, since the party would be confined mainly to the rear porch and backyard, in addition to the kitchen. Yards of crepe paper in those same colors still had to be hung, along with the attractively stenciled Happy Birthday sign that would cover one long kitchen wall.

A far-from-small donkey covered in sequins would hardly fit in. Anything but.

Her companion's only response to her less-than-enthusiastic comment was to rip open a bag of pretzels and extend it her way. "Want some?"

"No...thank you." As she had days earlier when they'd discussed the menu, Abby found herself groping for patience. "You didn't have to buy this many snacks, you know. We don't need them, or certainly not this much, not with all the other food."

Ryan bit into a pretzel with a crunch and polished it off in short order. "Maybe you women don't need them," he said, "but from the guest list you showed me, several men are coming to this party along with a bunch of Ethel's lady friends."

"And none of the group will probably be much under sixty," Abby reminded him. "Most will be around Ethel's age—or maybe even older. This is basically a seniors' get-together, not a Super Bowl party." And because of that, it would wind up early. In fact, she had little doubt that by ten o'clock the whole thing would be over. "We're going to have mounds of leftovers if we put everything out."

"I'm willing to risk it," Ryan replied easily. "Now, why don't we hang up the decorations? Then you can get dressed for the big event while I load a cooler with soda and beer and watch out for any new bed and breakfast customers. When you come back downstairs, you can make the fancy sandwiches and whatever, plus the punch, while I take a shower and get dressed. Then we'll both be ready to deal with the party guests when they start getting here."

"Okay," Abby murmured after a moment, failing to find anything lacking in that suggestion. "I don't expect any of the people who have weekend reservations at Aunt Abigail's to arrive for at least another hour."

"Good," Ryan said. "We should have this place decorated in time for you to get dressed before the first of them shows up to check in. If not, I can entertain them for a few minutes. It won't be any trouble."

"Right." It seemed only reasonable to her to agree. How could she not when he was being so helpful? True, he hadn't gone along entirely with her plans, but that was hardly cause to start dragging her heels now. And besides, there was no time to waste. "Let's get started," she said, squaring her shoulders. "We have a lot to do."

Once again that odd little smile curved the corners of his mouth. "Don't worry," he told her. "It will all work out. Everything's under control."

EVERYTHING WAS indeed under control, Abby decided a few hours later as she and Ryan waited in the kitchen doorway for the first of the birthday guests to arrive. Those who were driving had already been instructed to park along the wide alley bordering the backyard, and all had been asked to come in via the rear gate and enter the house through the back-porch door. Everyone scheduled to arrive for weekend stays at the bed and breakfast had been checked in, and most had since departed for dinner armed with Abby's restaurant recommendations.

Only the dapper Major Hobbs, who was still with them, had been invited to the party, since he and Ethel seemed to enjoy each other's company. The veteran army man had said he would be "delighted to attend" in his smooth Southern accent. He had even offered to act as lookout at the front window, ready to raise the alarm when the Stocktons returned with Cara and Ethel.

Her earlier wariness now seemed foolish, Abby had to admit. Yes, a glittering donkey hung from a low tree branch in the backyard and heaping bowls of snacks rested on several small tables placed around the party area, but her own plans had proceeded without a hitch. A platter filled with a variety of finger sandwiches held center stage on the kitchen table, with a large crystal bowl of fizzy, orange-flavored punch occupying one side and trays of cut vegetables, cheese and crackers on the other.

A job well done, Abby told herself in silent congratulation as she smoothed a hand down the front of one of the few dresses she'd brought with her to Harmony. Made of bottle-green silk, it featured a rounded neckline, long, fitted sleeves and a wide, midcalf-length skirt. She wore low-heeled pumps, and the cut of the dress was plain enough to make it just a notch above casual, which she imagined would fit in with whatever the rest of the group opted to wear.

For his part, Ryan had chosen a banded-collar, Western-style white shirt with thin pleats running down the front and a pair of slim-legged black pants. And as simple as that outfit was, Abby thought, slanting a glance his way, he looked even more dangerously attractive than usual. She wished the guests would get here. They'd been alone for too long to suit her.

"The weather turned out to be perfect," she said, seeking some casual conversation to break a short stretch of silence. "It must be at least seventy degrees right now, and not a cloud in the sky."

"It'll get chilly later, though," Ryan reminded her as he lounged against the doorjamb, arms crossed over his chest. "Once the sun goes down, the temperature seems to drop fairly quick here at this time of the year."

Abby shrugged. "Well, I'm sure everyone knows enough to bring a jacket or sweater. In any case, the party will probably be long over before it gets too cool outside."

He lifted an eyebrow. "You think so?"

"Don't you?" she asked, wondering why he looked far from convinced of something that appeared to be almost a given to her.

However he might have answered, their conversation was cut short as the first two guests arrived. Fortunately Abby already knew both, since they had attended her godmother's wedding.

"Nice to see you again," Tom Kennedy, Harmony's longtime police chief, said in an easygoing drawl that seemed to come naturally to him. He quickly tipped his wide-brimmed tan hat, barely revealing a receding hairline before he settled it back on his head.

The petite lady with one delicately boned hand resting on the chief's arm had to be close to twenty years his senior, but that hadn't dimmed the shrewd intelligence sparkling in clear blue eyes framed by gold-rimmed glasses. Miss Hester Goodbody, Abby had already learned, was a veteran first-grade teacher who had taught scores of Harmony residents. Now, gently nodding her silver-haired head, the elderly woman said in the warmest of tones, "Why, of course, it's wonderful to see you again, my dear."

Abby greeted them both, and then introduced Ryan as a current resident of Aunt Abigail's, deciding to let them come to their own conclusions as to what that meant, because she had no intention of mentioning their past relationship.

"Call me Miss Hester," the teacher told Ryan after handshakes were completed. "Everyone does."

Ryan smiled down at her. "I'll do that."

Miss Hester's eyes twinkled. "Oh, my. You're a handsome lad when you smile."

"Now, don't fuss over him too much or I'll get jealous," Tom warned in a gruff voice.

Both guests shared a brief laugh over that before Abby invited them into the kitchen and offered refreshments. Tom wasted no time in opting for a beer, which Ryan produced in short order from a large cooler standing near the refrigerator.

Miss Hester viewed the items on the table. Her sharp gaze seemed to miss nothing. "Everything looks delicious," she said at last, straightening one edge of the crocheted, ecru shawl draped over her dark blue shirtwaist dress. "I believe I'll have some punch to start."

Abby dipped a crystal ladle in the mixture, poured a small glassful and handed it over just as a group of other guests arrived. "Excuse me," she said and walked forward to greet them.

After that things happened quickly. In a matter of minutes the rear of the house was filled with people chatting in the way of longtime friends. Those still in the kitchen halted their conversations when Major Hobbs, wearing a trim gray sport coat with charcoal trousers, popped in to make an announcement.

"Ladies and gentlemen, the guest of honor is arriving," he said with characteristic old-fashioned courtesy. "The car has just pulled into the driveway, so I recommend everyone find a hiding place."

People scattered all around at that news, and Abby made one last check of the kitchen to make sure things were in order. Satisfied, she walked to the wall switch and snapped off the overhead light, plunging the room into the murky shadows of early twilight. As she'd explained to the guests, Bill and Gail would gradually steer Ethel in here. One of the Stocktons would switch the light back on, and that would be the signal for everyone to reappear.

Having already chosen her hiding spot earlier that day, one close enough to ensure her own rapid reappearance, she stepped over to a small closet built into the wall near the kitchen entrance, pulled the door open, slipped inside and shut the door behind her.

And then she discovered she wasn't alone.

Coming up against a rock-solid body as she inched forward in total darkness was enough to tell her that in no uncertain terms. And not just any body. Oh, no. She didn't have to see to know who it was.

All she had to do was feel.

"Fancy meeting you here," Ryan said, his tone wry with an easy familiarity. He'd either caught a glimpse of her slipping in or he had recognized her as she had him—by sheer touch.

Abby immediately inched away again, only to come up against the door. Even with her spine pressed to it, she couldn't put much distance between them. "This was supposed to be my spot to hide."

"Too bad you didn't mention that."

Hadn't she? No, with everything else going on, she'd never given a thought to staking a claim. And now it was too late to be out searching for another spot. "Yes, well, maybe you could move back slightly," she suggested, "and give us both a little space."

"Afraid not," he replied, his voice even deeper than usual, as if resounding off the narrow walls. "I've got what you might say is a real close acquaintance going on with a bunch of cleaning utensils at the moment. Guess we'll just have to tough it out until the kitchen light pops on."

Abby sighed softly. "We may not even know when that happens," she pointed out, "unless I can get turned around enough to peek out the door."

"Uh-huh," he muttered. "Good luck."

Firmly suspecting she would need it, Abby drew

her arms in close to her body and gave it a try. It didn't take long for her shoulder to bump straight into his side, and both objects refused to budge.

"I think I heard something," Ryan said just then, his mouth near her ear.

Abby stilled completely. "Could be the front door opening. Don't make a sound," she told him.

And he didn't. Maybe that's why it suddenly seemed all too quiet in their small temporary prison. Quiet enough to have time taking on a dimension of its own as the silence built between them. More than quiet enough to have tight threads of an unmistakable tension that had nothing to do with the event about to take place rising to surround them.

They couldn't see, couldn't speak, couldn't move.

All they could do was wait.

And wait.

Abby wasn't sure who broke first, it happened so quickly. One second they were standing as still as statues and the next their lips were locked together.

A bare instant later their arms were wrapped around each other and they were kissing, tasting, touching like there was no tomorrow. Or yesterday.

Live for the moment—this moment, their bodies seemed to be saying even as they let wandering hands have their way and all but wound themselves into one person, pressing closer and closer. And then closer still.

With a low groan, he cupped his palms around her hips and tugged her flat against him. With a soft moan, she fisted her fingers in his hair and held on tight. Both emerged from the kiss for a moment, breathing fast and hard.

Then they began to do it all over again.

And that was when a chorus of shouts melded into a single, ringing statement.

"Surprise!"

Chapter Six

Ryan was still trying to rally his thought processes when Abby pulled away from him. Her back met the door with a small thud. Once again their labored breaths mingled in the darkness before he managed to speak.

"I think the party's started without us," he said in a husky whisper.

Abby moaned again. This time it was clear that no passion was involved. "We have to get out of here," she told him, her voice hushed yet urgent.

"Maybe you do," he conceded, "but I'd better stay put for a minute. If anyone got a good look at me right now, they might wind up a lot more surprised than Ethel."

Clearly getting his drift, Abby swallowed hard enough to be heard and drew in another deep breath. "All right," she said. "I'll just slip out as quietly as possible."

"You do that."

She did, backing away and easing herself out just as the group began to sing "Happy Birthday." The mingled voices faded slightly as the door closed again behind her.

"Okay, Larabee," Ryan muttered to himself. "It's time to get a grip."

He lifted his hands and ran them through his hair, straightening it as best he could while his breathing gradually slowed and his body started to calm down. Not that it wanted to. No, it would far rather he hauled Abby back into the closet without delay and took things to their natural conclusion.

Too bad that wasn't an option.

Ryan waited until a round of applause went up after a second chorus of the birthday tune before he opened the door and quickly slipped out. Luckily everyone seemed to have their attention fixed on the guest of honor, who stood near the kitchen table beaming a wide smile at her companions.

"Now I know why I was talked into wearing this outfit home." She dropped a pleased glance down at her new teal pantsuit, then lifted a small glass of punch in a toast. "This is to friends. I have some of the best, and I'm so glad you're all here."

With that, the party began in earnest, and Ryan wasted no time in heading for the cooler and a beer. He couldn't deny he needed one. His pulse was still a long way from steady. After a lengthy swallow, he wound his way through the crowd and started toward the back porch, getting a glimpse of Abby on his way. She was holding Cara and talking to several of the guests. The baby, all decked out in a pastel-print dress and fluffy white sweater was grinning from tiny ear to tiny ear, but Abby's calm expression was unreadable.

Whatever she thought about the closet episode, she wasn't sending out any signals.

Ryan found an open spot along the wide porch window and leaned against the glass, preferring to stand even though a few chairs were available because his backside had taken another beating from the bull that morning. And as many times as he'd dusted himself off and got back on, he still hadn't lasted more than five seconds before Lively had sent him sprawling.

Grimacing briefly, Ryan glanced out at the view. A string of small lanterns lit the yard, glowing more brightly as night approached. Only a few guests had ventured outside so far, and they were gathered by the round, two-tiered stone fountain.

He saw no one he could put a name to. Not that he hadn't been introduced, but there were too many visitors for him to keep names straight. They didn't have the same problem, though, and several stopped by where he stood to trade casual comments. Harmony had definitely turned out to be a friendly place, he reflected, recalling what he'd been told before his arrival.

The fact that at least some of its residents knew how to enjoy themselves soon became apparent, as well. Major inroads had been made on the food, Ryan noted with a stop at the kitchen table on his first trip to replenish snack supplies. The punch bowl was down by more than half, too. The radio resting on the counter, tuned to the same station as another radio on the porch, sent out a stream of golden-oldies music, and a few couples had already slow-danced to some doo-wop favorites.

The party, Ryan concluded with satisfaction, was going well.

By the time Ethel tackled the piñata, she'd gotten into the spirit of the evening enough to slice off the donkey's rear with one enthusiastic whack of a long broom handle. Wrapped hard candies spilled out in a colorful waterfall and landed on a blanket spread under the tree. A rousing cheer went up, but Ethel didn't stop there. She took off the donkey's head with another swipe, a feat many of her lady friends plainly found hilarious. They whooped with laughter and bent over, holding their sides.

Bill Stockton slipped next to where Ryan stood in a far corner of the yard. "How much booze did you put in the punch?" he asked in a mild undertone as they both viewed the women.

Ryan folded his arms across his chest. "Believe it or not, less than a cup of vodka for the whole bowlful."

Bill's chuckle came from low in his throat. "Most of these ladies indulge in a glass of wine on occasion. They don't exactly have a close acquaintance with hard liquor."

"Yeah," Ryan muttered, "I'm beginning to see that."

And he was, watching as the town's veteran schoolteacher wasted no time in tossing her shawl to another elderly woman before she tried her luck with the broom handle. One of the donkey's legs went flying.

"Good thing Tom Kennedy and I switched to soda a while back," Bill said. "It looks as though Miss Hester won't be the only one Tom will be driving home tonight, and I'll probably have my share to drop off on the way back to my place. Even Major Hobbs seems to be getting into the swing of things."

Ryan studied the man who stood beside the porch steps viewing the proceedings with an indulgent smile curving his lips, his thin mustache a dark contrast to the silver streaks at his temples.

"What do you think of the major?" Ryan asked, slanting his gaze toward Bill.

"Haven't had a chance to talk to him for more than a few minutes, but he seems to be a nice sort," the older man readily replied. "Abby and Ethel like him."

"I know," Ryan said.

Bill lifted an eyebrow as his eyes met Ryan's. "And you don't?"

"I can't really say that."

Which was the total truth, Ryan thought. He and the major had shared several conversations since the ex-army officer had shown up at Aunt Abigail's only days after his own arrival. Their discussions had generally focused on other spots of interest the well-traveled man had visited since his retirement and had never touched on anything even remotely personal—a fact that had suited his listener down to the ground when it came to maintaining his own privacy, Ryan reminded himself.

And if it also suited the major, why should that raise any questions? It shouldn't, was the obvious answer.

But somehow it did.

Ryan exhaled a short breath. "There's just something about him that has me reserving judgment—don't ask me what."

"Hmm." Bill mulled the matter over for a second. "How long does he plan on staying?"

"Hasn't said exactly. He keeps rebooking for another week. Says he likes this town too much to leave just yet, which could well be true, but..."

"But for some reason you've formed the notion that something's off," Bill summed up when Ryan hesitated. He frowned thoughtfully. "You know, it might not be a bad idea if our police chief spent a little time checking out a few things about the major. Tom and I go back a long way. He'd do it if I asked, and keep it quiet, too."

"Could be I'm dead wrong," Ryan pointed out.

"Could be," Bill conceded. "Even if that's how it plays out, though, it wouldn't hurt for me to take a peek at the information listed for him in the guest register and put a word in Tom's ear."

Ryan nodded after a moment. "Guess it wouldn't hurt," he said, and then switched his gaze back to the still-laughing ladies who had formed a line to take shots at what had once resembled a donkey. "Right now," he added dryly, "a little liquor appears to be going a long way."

The party kept going, as well, and only seemed to pick up speed as the evening wore on.

By the time a large whipped-cream cake topped with a blaze of candles was set out, a whole bunch of guests wanted to sing "Happy Birthday" again, and a good many accomplished the task loudly enough to have dogs in neighboring yards chiming in with eager howls.

By the time the Elvis impersonator showed up dressed in bad-boy black leather and sporting an impressive pair of sideburns, most people were ready to dance along with him as he twirled Ethel around the back porch in a mean jitterbug. When he left after favoring his partner with a soulful "Love Me Tender," the rest kept on dancing as the radio was turned up again. It didn't matter that the females outnumbered the males. The women danced together, and did a good job of it, too.

Ryan thought about giving it a try himself, but the only person he wanted to twirl around was staunchly keeping her distance. He doubted that Abby had come within six feet of him since they'd parted in the closet. So instead of dancing he opted for another beer and bumped into Bill again in the kitchen.

"Any more pretzels?" Bill asked as he helped himself to a can of soda from the cooler Ryan had restocked throughout the evening.

"Uh-uh. The pretzels are history. Same goes for the chips and dips. And just about everything else," Ryan said with a glance at the nearly empty plates covering the table. "This crowd sure knows how to eat. I guess it's time to pop some more popcorn." He looked at Bill. "Any idea as to when they'll decide to go home?"

Bill shook his head. "Right now, the only thing I'd be willing to say for certain is that my wife is flat-out sure to get her wish. This party is well on its way to being one to remember. Hell, it may wind up being famous."

ABBY FINALLY got to bed well after midnight, and the sun came up far too soon to suit her. Cara, with a good night's rest behind her, since she'd headed for dreamland before the party was half-over, babbled in her crib as Abby struggled to get moving. She took a quick shower while the baby was still content to amuse herself, then dressed in one of her tailored blouses along with pleated slacks. Feeling marginally more awake, she entered the small bedroom next to her own and was greeted by a cheerfully shouted welcome.

"Ma!" Cara sat straight up and held her chubby arms out wide.

Smiling, Abby lifted the baby from a snowy-white crib decorated with tiny painted animals, then pressed a kiss down on Cara's silky dark curls. "Good morning. Let's do a diaper change, little dickens, and then we'll make you some breakfast."

It was still early when Abby entered the kitchen with the baby in her arms, but Ethel was there, wearing one of her ruffled aprons and humming an upbeat tune as she rolled out biscuit dough with skillful strokes. Abby blinked at the sight, well aware that the older woman had been up as late as, and partied far more than, she herself had.

"I'm in awe," she didn't hesitate to admit. "You look terrific while I feel like I should search for some toothpicks to prop up my eyelids."

Ethel's smile was just a little bit smug. "My generation has stamina, dear."

"It must." Abby settled Cara on one hip. "I don't have to ask if you had a good time last night, either. It was clear you did."

"I can't wait to tell my daughter all about it," Ethel said. "It was so thoughtful of everyone to make the day so special. I hope you had a good time, too."

"Mmm-hmm," Abby murmured in a deliberately neutral response, since that hadn't been the case, not entirely. Not with the continual effort she'd had to make to put the closet incident behind her so she could be a gracious hostess to Ethel's friends without anyone suspecting that it *was* an effort.

Ethel cleared her throat delicately. "Hester Goodbody said you looked a little, ah, flustered when you popped out of the kitchen closet.''

Oh, no. Abby resisted the urge to wince, barely. *So much for slipping out quietly,* she told herself. Obviously that didn't work when a sharp-eyed schoolteacher was around. Nevertheless, she knew it could be worse. Miss Hester could have seen—

''She also said Ryan was looking a bit strange when he came out,'' Ethel added in the most casual of tones.

Now Abby did wince. She couldn't help it. ''Yes, well, it wasn't all that comfortable in there. Not that we planned on crowding in together. It just happened that way.''

''I see,'' Ethel said with a distinct sparkle in her eye before she started humming again and went back to her task.

More than willing to let the subject drop, Abby set Cara on the floor and left her to crawl to a favorite spot under the table while she fixed cereal. The last thing she wanted to talk about was what had taken place in that closet. She didn't even want to think about it.

But there, she knew she had no choice. Not after the way she and Ryan had wound themselves around each other. By mutual consent, too. At least it would be considered consent, she reflected, if any thinking had been involved. For her part, she had no recollection of making a conscious choice.

It had just...happened.

But she'd certainly participated to the hilt once things got going, and sooner or later she had to come to terms with that fact. *It had better be sooner, too,* a niggling voice in the back of her mind said, *because*

*you're still engaged—and not to the man you were
wound around.*

"I wish Allan had been able to come to the party,"
Abby said, and fully meant it. If he had, she would
have found a hiding place with him and that small
voice of guilt wouldn't be nagging at her now.

"I don't think he would have enjoyed it all that
much, dear," Ethel replied.

Abby looked at her. "Why?"

"He just strikes me as the more reserved type. I'm
sure he enjoys attending a social occasion now and
then, but not the kind we had last night."

Abby had to wonder if that were true. Probably,
she conceded after a thoughtful moment. Although
Allan was friendly enough and outgoing in his own
conservative way, he no doubt would have preferred
the quiet get-together she'd planned on rather than the
kind of party it had turned into, much to her amazement.

The kind of party Ethel and her friends had loved,
she couldn't deny, and the one that Ryan Larabee had
surely had a hand in accomplishing. She didn't need
to wring a confession out of him to see his finger-
prints all over the evening's surprising events.

To her, it was one more telling indication that he
and Allan were as different as night and day. And she
had chosen Allan.

Keeping that firmly in mind until she saw her fiancé again was the wisest thing to do, Abby decided.
When they met face-to-face and she could look into
his eyes, she would know whether she had made the
right decision in agreeing to marry him. She had to
believe that. And she did.

In the meantime, it could only be smart, not to

mention less stressful on her already overworked nerves, to redouble the efforts she'd made last night to maintain a cautious distance when it came to—

"I need coffee," Ryan said just then as he entered the kitchen. He wore jeans with a denim shirt left hanging to drop past his waist and sported a night's growth of beard. His bare feet moved silently on the tile as he headed for the dark mixture Ethel had already brewed.

Abby could have used some herself, but that wouldn't have served her current purposes, and she was a determined woman. Moving with hard-won efficiency, she placed a bowl of cereal on the table, reached down to lift Cara into her lap and started feeding the baby, who wasted no time in falling in with Abby's plan to get the job done quickly. She wanted to head back upstairs and give Cara a bath, after which she intended to be very busy for the rest of the day and all day Sunday. And even after the weekend guests were gone, there must be plenty to do away from Aunt Abigail's.

Away from *him*.

She could spend her mornings helping Ethel with whatever needed to be done here and her afternoons becoming more acquainted with the city. If nothing else, the fresh air would do both her and Cara good.

And when Allan drove up on Friday evening, she had to hope she would have no qualms about coming to the swift conclusion that she had made the right choice.

"You can't be as bright-eyed and bushy-tailed as you look," Ryan said just then, drawing Abby's attention to where he leaned against the counter, coffee mug in hand. She knew even before noting the direction of his gaze that he couldn't mean her.

Ethel kept spreading newly cut biscuit circles on a large baking sheet and smiled another smug smile. "My generation," she said for the second time that morning, "has stamina."

"Uh-huh," Ryan murmured. "Maybe if I'm patient, I'll wind up with some."

SEVERAL DAYS LATER patience was the last thing on Ryan's mind as he hauled himself up off the ground and blew out a disgusted breath. "*Six* seconds? After eating dust for four fun-filled mornings, all I'm up to is six blasted seconds?"

Bill thumbed back his hat and gazed down at his companion from his seat on top of the corral fence. "I only call it like my stopwatch sees it. And Lively seems to agree, because he's still turning his nose up at you."

Ryan bent and brushed off his jeans. "Don't remind me," he said. The fact that it had just happened again, after which the bull had thrown in the towel and calmly headed for the barn, was surely enough to have most men groping for a grip on their temper. Right now, his was hanging by a thread.

At least he hadn't been the one to call an end to today's session, Ryan thought, although he probably would've had to soon if the bull hadn't decided to beat him to it. A few portions of his body were beyond sore at the moment. They had actually gone numb.

Ryan hobbled over to Bill. "What the hell does that animal do when someone does manage to stay on his back for the full eight seconds?"

Bill smiled his wily smile. "I'll leave it to you to find out. Just don't wait too long on it. The rodeo's ten days away."

"I know, trust me. The last weekend in May."

Bill's expression sobered. "Have you come up with any more thoughts on what else might be happening then?"

Ryan shook his head. "This damn blank wall in my mind still isn't budging an inch."

And as frustrating as that was, he had to admit that something else was bothering him even more at the moment. It was another kind of wall—the invisible one Abby kept shored up between them whenever they were in seeing distance of each other. At least that was what she'd seemed to be doing for the past few days. Then again, she hadn't been around much at all lately, not even within seeing range, so maybe that you-may-be-looking-straight-at-me-but-I'm-not-really-here wall of determined indifference was purely a product of his imagination.

But he didn't think so.

And he missed her. He even missed butting heads with her over proper party food. He couldn't deny it, and that's what really stuck in his craw. He was missing her, while she probably couldn't wait for the week to end so her fiancé could tear himself away from his doctor duties long enough to drive up and put an engagement ring on her finger.

Cripes, you are one sad case, Larabee.

Bill hopped down from the fence and landed with a soft thud. "You got enough energy left to help me put the new screen door on the house?" he asked, arching a brow.

"As long as I don't have to sit down to do it, I'm game," Ryan said.

Bill laughed, a hearty sound in the quiet landscape all around them. "Maybe I can round up some liniment for you to take back to Aunt Abigail's."

Which would be a terrific idea if he could convince a certain woman to give him a private rubdown. Ryan had to laugh himself knowing the chances of that happening were zip. She'd more likely pour it over his head if he even suggested it. He tugged the brim of his hat down a notch over his eyes and fell into step with Bill as they left the corral through a side gate and started toward the house.

"I haven't heard from our police chief yet on what he's been able to find out about the major," Bill remarked, "but he said it could take a little while."

Ryan slid his hands into his pockets and thought about the recent breakfasts he'd shared with the former military man, something that had become more or less a habit, since they'd been the only guests around on the weekdays. As an experiment, he'd tried easing the conversation into more personal lines a few times, but the major had even more smoothly eased it back to general subjects.

Suspicious behavior? Not when you considered that everyone was entitled to their privacy, Ryan had to admit. "I hope the chief will take it in stride if it winds up being a waste of time," he said.

"No problem," Bill assured him. "Tom Kennedy may seem like the easygoing sort, but he doesn't take his job lightly, and he'd just as soon go to a bit of trouble now than let it ride and possibly end up sorry later."

"I suppose that's the smart attitude to take." Ryan

kicked a stray piece of gravel and unintentionally sent it soaring to land several yards away.

"Uh-huh. And speaking of smart…" Bill hesitated for a beat. "After we get this door on, it might be wise if you considered finding a way to take an edge off the frustration that's standing out all over you."

Ryan launched a sidelong look. "And here I figured I was hiding it so well."

Ignoring the ripe irony in that statement, Bill said, "It's your business, of course, but you just might end up blowing a gasket."

"And what do you suggest I do?" Ryan asked, forcing himself to ease up on the sarcasm.

Bill shrugged. "Take a drive up into the mountains, maybe. We don't get much rain here this time of year and it's another beauty of a day, in case you hadn't noticed. Perfect opportunity to treat yourself to a good look at nature. Or if you'd rather head back toward town instead, Harmony Park is smack-dab in the middle of the city. Walk around there for a while. Hell, you could even feed the ducks."

What he'd really rather do was kick a stubborn bull in the butt. Or, better still, kiss the bejeezus out of the former Mrs. Larabee. Yeah, that would be way better.

A whole lot better, Ryan thought, than feeding ducks.

"Dut!"

Abby grinned down at Cara from her seat on a small blanket stretched out in the shade of a tall oak. "That's pretty close to *duck*, little dickens. Good job."

The baby didn't so much as glance up at her,

clearly fascinated by the activity taking place in the deep blue waters of the park lagoon a short distance from where they sat. It was a picture-perfect scene, Abby had to concede. The golden sun shining off the water, the brown ducks darting back and forth, swimming to the tune of their own special chatter, people of all ages strolling by enjoying a peaceful afternoon outdoors.

Abby was enjoying it, too.

She had, in fact, enjoyed the past few afternoons far more than she'd expected. It had been good for both her and Cara to spend some time together, just the two of them. Playing tourist before the busy summer season arrived, they'd investigated a few of the family-oriented sites the city had to offer, and there were many.

Harmony was indeed a good place to raise a child. Her godmother had been right about that, Abby couldn't help but acknowledge. And the place held definite rewards for adults, as well—the first and foremost being the genuinely sociable atmosphere.

"Great party!" she'd been told by several now-familiar residents she'd run into in the busier downtown area or passed on the quieter neighborhood streets. And they'd always said it with a smile.

"Thanks. Glad you had a good time," she'd replied again and again, smiling her own small smile at the knowledge that they probably should have reserved their comments for another person entirely. The person who knew—who had always known—how to throw a—

Just then Abby's thoughts scattered as that same person—the very person she knew full well it would be wiser not to even think about—abruptly moved into her field of vision as he walked along the banks of the lagoon. Today, together with his usual blue denim and black Stetson, he wore a sober expression much closer to a scowl than a smile.

Ryan Larabee was obviously not enjoying his afternoon.

Which might be to her advantage, Abby told herself. Maybe he wouldn't spot her, the way he seemed to be thoroughly caught up in whatever he was pondering. Perhaps ''brooding over'' would be a better description. She didn't plan on bringing her presence to his attention, that was certain. Facing him across the dinner table every evening was about the only time she really saw him anymore, and as far as she was concerned, dinnertime was soon enough to get a close-up view of him today. More than soon enough.

But then he spotted her, his gaze narrowing as recognition hit. He still looked a long way from smiling as he climbed a gentle slope and approached the blanket. Cara kept her attention firmly fixed on the ducks, as though she hadn't even noticed him. Abby wished she could cope with his arrival half as easily. Oh, for the joys of childhood.

''Mind if I sit down?'' he asked.

''No,'' she said after the barest pause. And really what else could she say? *Go away, because I'm not up to dealing with my former husband while I'm waiting for my current fiancé to get here so I can look into his eyes and discover if I made a mistake?*

Not hardly. She wasn't sharing that news with anyone.

Ryan sat on the edge of the blanket, bent his long legs and propped his forearms on his knees. ''Nice day,'' he muttered by way of conversation.

"Mmm-hmm." Abby was in no mood to smile herself, not now, but she kept her tone polite. "Ethel told me that in a few months afternoon thunderstorms will roll in even more frequently here than they do in Phoenix during the summer."

"Humph," was his only reply to that as he reached up to remove his hat and set it on the grass beside him.

Cara said even less as she pulled herself to her feet and placed a little hand on Abby's shoulder to keep herself upright. She never took her attention off the lagoon, her eyes as saucer-round as those displayed by the tiny teddy bears dotting her playsuit. The swimming ducks were evidently fascinating.

"Do you want to talk about it?" Ryan asked abruptly, winning Abby's full attention in a heartbeat. He didn't need to elaborate to have her sure what *it* was. One glimpse of the probing gleam that had sparked to life in his gaze spoke volumes.

"I think," she replied deliberately, "that it would be better not to dwell on what took place in that closet."

"Are you blaming me?" Again the question was blunt.

"No." Sheer honesty forced her to admit it had been a mutual thing. Wildly foolish, undoubtedly. But mutual. "I was as responsible for that particular incident as you were."

He heaved a gusty sigh. "Well, I'm glad we at least got that straight."

Yes, it was probably good they had, Abby decided, feeling some of her own tension ease. Maybe after owning up to what she had done, she could truly put the matter behind her and—

"Dut! Dut! Dut!"

The sudden shouts rang in Abby's ears even as she realized Cara no longer stood beside her. Much to her shock, she saw that the baby was making straight for the lagoon, to where one of the smaller ducks had drifted in close to shore. Just like that, Cara was walking on her own for the very first time, then running as she picked up speed heading down the slope.

"Oh, my God!" Abby cried as she shot to her feet. "She's going to fall in the water."

And then Cara did exactly that.

Chapter Seven

Ryan had his boots off in a flash. Abby was still at the edge of the bank frantically toeing off her own shoes when he raced past her and executed a shallow dive. The ducks sent up a round of squawks as he hit the surface. He barely heard them before he went under. As he'd expected, the water was fairly deep and undeniably cold. Thankfully, it was also clear.

He had no trouble locating the baby. Arms and legs flailing, she was sending up a stream of small bubbles and spinning helplessly. One swift stroke took him to her, then she was locked in his grip and they were both surging to the surface. They'd barely broken through the water when she started crying at the top of her lungs.

When they reached the grassy bank moments later, quiet tears were rolling down Abby's cheeks, as well. Other concerned faces had joined hers, watching as Ryan used one arm to tug himself half out of the water while keeping the other securely around Cara. Abby quickly bent to take the baby, but the sturdy little arms that had captured Ryan's neck in a choke-hold refused to budge.

"Let her stay," he finally said over the baby's nonstop stop wails, and at that point two men in the small crowd that had gathered acted with dispatch and gained a firm grip on his leather belt. Legs braced at the edge of the water, they lifted Ryan and his burden onto the bank.

"We have to get those wet clothes off her," Abby said, her voice trembling as she knelt beside him. She already had the blanket in her hands, which were trembling as well.

Ryan had to pry Cara's arms from his neck so they could get the job done. Once the baby was wrapped in the blanket and snug in Abby's lap, he stripped off his shirt and socks, pulled on the black boots someone had retrieved for him and got to his feet. And still Cara cried, wrestling the blanket off enough to reach out to him.

"It might be better if I hold her," he said. He bent to lift the child, blanket and all, and once her arms were locked around his neck again, the crying soon faded to sobs.

Abby picked up the dripping clothing he'd discarded. "I'm taking her to the medical center downtown," she told him. "I don't intend to take any chances."

He nodded. "Fine. I'll drive you. My car's in the lot near the main park entrance."

"That silver bullet you drive may go fast, but it's too small to hold all of us," she reminded him. "We'll have to use my car. It's parked in the lot, too."

While Ryan thanked the bystanders for their help, Abby grabbed up his hat and her shoulder bag. It wasn't long before they reached her late-model sedan, where it became apparent that Cara had no intention of letting Ryan hand her over to Abby so he could drive. Every time he tried to ease her away, she started crying again. And not softly.

"Guess she's going to scream bloody murder if I'm not in touching distance," Ryan said at last.

Which came as a surprise, he had to admit. Nothing in his background, at least as much of it as he'd been able to piece together so far, indicated he was anywhere near an expert when it came to children. In fact, he had to wonder if he had ever held a baby before today. Somehow he doubted it. Now that the chief crisis was over, and he had time to think about it, holding this small bundle in his arms didn't feel at all familiar to him. Many of the things he'd attempted since the accident seemed to come naturally to him, as swimming had minutes ago. This was different.

"Why don't you get in the back with her?" Abby suggested. "I'll drive."

He frowned. "Are you okay to drive?" Some color had returned to her face, he noticed, conducting a short study. Her ivory blouse and beige slacks had undeniably seen better days; both were streaked with water and sported thin smears of dirt. But her hands no longer trembled.

"I can do it," she said, her voice steady now, as well. "It's not far, either. Just a few blocks."

"Okay."

He got in with the baby, who wailed again while she was strapped into her car seat. But once Ryan put an arm around her and held her close, she stopped. Just like that. It wasn't only surprising, he decided. It was flat-out amazing.

Abby pulled into a wide driveway leading to a three-story white-brick building in a matter of minutes. "I'm going to the emergency entrance," she said, aiming a look at Ryan in the rearview mirror. "They may send us back to the main lobby, but it seems like a good place to start."

Cara cried again, sobbing this time rather than screaming, when Ryan shifted away to release her from the car seat and Abby worked fast to put on a new diaper. Then she quieted as soon as Ryan lifted her out. He looked up at the sign on the building.

"Hayward Medical Center," he read out loud as Abby joined him at the entrance. "There's a Hayward Street, too, that I drove down to get to the park."

"The Haywards are one of Harmony's founding families," Abby told him.

"Must be another news bulletin you heard courtesy of Ethel," he said, making his tone wry. He couldn't deny that he was glad to see it produce a real, if faint, smile. It seemed like forever since this woman had smiled a genuine smile at him. Maybe not since the night she'd cheerfully informed him of her agreement to marry another man. *I said yes.*

Well, he wasn't letting that particular subject get to him any longer, Ryan decided as they entered the emergency area. It was time to back off. If she wanted Dr. Wonderful despite what had happened on the evening of Ethel's party, then she did, and that was that. He supposed he could be as sensitive as the next guy and support her right to make her own choices. And he would. Dammit.

ONE LOOK at the doctor who saw them after only a short delay and Abby sensed they were in good hands. The middle-aged woman with short, ebony hair and fine, cocoa-brown skin seemed to radiate a quiet confidence in her own abilities even as she displayed a reassuring smile for the examination room's occupants. Far from aiming the slightest glance at Ryan's bare chest as he sat under the muted light of a frosted window—and the young nurse they'd first talked to had launched several—Dr. Eunice Thompson, as she introduced herself, quickly fixed her attention on her patient.

"Hello, sweetheart," she said softly. "I understand you took an unexpected dip in the lagoon today."

Demonstrating a shyness seldom evident before, the baby's only response was to put her little face in the crook of Ryan's muscled neck and hold on even more tightly to him.

"She's been having trouble letting go of me since I got her out of the water," he explained.

The doctor's smile grew. "I'd say she feels safe with you. You must be a good father."

"No, he's not," Abby blurted out, as startled by that last statement as the man in question surely had been. She hadn't missed the way he seemed taken aback for a second. "I mean, he's not her father." She took an instant to regain her composure. "The baby's name is Cara, I'm Abby Prentice, her legal guardian, and this is Ryan Larabee. He's a…friend of ours."

"I see," the doctor murmured, angling her head a notch as her gaze took on a shrewd sparkle, as if she suspected more might lurk behind the basic facts Abby had offered. "Why don't we try removing that blanket and sitting Cara up on the examination table?" she suggested, directing that comment to Ryan. "You can sit next to her."

"My jeans are still wet," he warned as Abby dealt

with pulling off the blanket to leave Cara decked only in her diaper. "I'm sure to get the table wet, too."

"It'll survive," the doctor assured him.

"Okay." He eased himself onto the table and let his legs hang down. Again he had to pry Cara's arms from his neck. Mournful sobs started, then quickly ceased as he propped her up beside him and placed a hand on the back of her head, where a riot of damp curls sprang in all directions.

The doctor nodded her approval. "I think that's a workable solution." She pushed up the sleeves of her white coat and began to conduct a gentle examination. "Did Cara lose consciousness at all?" she asked after a minute.

"No." Ryan's mouth quirked up at the tips. "In fact, she came up wailing for all she was worth."

"That's good," Dr. Thompson remarked as she listened to the baby's lungs.

"We got her right out of her wet clothes, too," Abby added.

"Then she probably didn't get too chilled. Everything considered, I don't believe there's much to worry about."

Abby issued a relieved sigh at the doctor's last words. Thank God, was all she could think. Thank God, the baby's first try at walking hadn't led to far worse consequences.

Then the man seated on the table shifted his gaze to meet hers, and she realized that someone else more than deserved a share of her gratitude. Someone who had wasted no time in coming to the rescue. "Thank *you*," she said softly.

Ryan shook his head. "No need to do that," he replied, his voice as soft as hers.

They broke eye contact when the doctor took a step back from her patient and spoke again. "You seem to be in tip-top shape, Cara." This time the baby dipped her little chin in a nod, as if seconding that statement. It won an amused laugh from the doctor before she turned to Abby. "My only caution would be to keep a lookout for signs of a fever tonight," she said. "If one develops that's more than a few degrees above normal, bring her back in."

"All right," Abby agreed. She handed the blanket back to Ryan and offered more thanks while he wrapped the baby up.

"You're certainly welcome." With that, the doctor leaned in slightly and dropped her voice to a confidential level. "My professional opinion, backed by my eyesight, is not to let your, ah, friend get away, Ms. Prentice. He's a—I believe the medical term would be—*stud.*"

It surprised an amused look out of Abby. "That's quite a diagnosis."

"Are we ready to go?" Ryan asked, viewing both women with an arched brow as he stood beside the table with Cara in his arms.

"Mmm-hmm," Abby said.

They left the doctor and walked out into crisp, clear sunshine. Abby drew in a breath of warm air that held a hint of the flowering bushes planted at the side of the building. "I'll drive back to the park so you can pick up your car," she said.

"This time I'll do the driving," Ryan countered. He looked sidelong at the baby. "The whole thing's over and there's no reason to be afraid anymore," he told her with confidence. "It's time to let someone else hold you. You gave her quite a scare, you know. In fact, you scared us both spitless.''

All at once Cara grinned from ear to ear, as though well pleased with that news. She gradually unwound her arms from Ryan's neck and leaned back to study him, then reached up to pat both of his hard cheeks lightly with her tiny hands.

''Pips!'' she declared, and patted him again.

Ryan's lips curved in a wry smile. ''Pips, is it? Well, I guess you've still got me confused with somebody's granddaddy, but it's a whole lot better than...what you were calling me, you little devil.'' To which comment the baby giggled in response, prompting Ryan's own deep chuckle.

Abby didn't follow their example, suddenly a long way from laughing as she took in the sight and sound of their exchange. For several seconds all she could do was stare. Then Cara turned and reached for her, and she found herself hugging a small body to her breasts and closing her eyes in sheer gratitude for the fact that Cara was truly safe.

Yet, even as the baby sighed and snuggled closer, the scene Abby had just viewed lingered in her mind, a vivid image that refused to dim. She had to wonder if she would ever completely forget it. The way the late-day sun had cast a glow over man and child. The way they had seemed to share that golden moment.

And the way she'd felt, watching them.

At the very core of her, something had stirred. Something she'd thought had long since faded to a mere memory of what had once been and would never be again. But she'd been wrong.

Abby gave a soundless sigh accepting both her error and the reality of what it meant. How could she not when it was suddenly so plain to her?

The unmistakable and undeniable truth was that the forceful attraction between her and the man who had reappeared from her past went beyond the pure physical awareness evident almost from the day he'd arrived in Harmony. Now she recognized her emotions were involved, as well.

Deep down, she still cared.

It was impossible to avoid that conclusion, and equally impossible not to realize how grossly unfair it would be to another man if she were to let him put a ring on her finger. Her conscience, which was as healthy as ever, simply wouldn't allow it, any more than it would let her even consider taking the easy way out and dealing with it over the telephone. She had to face him.

When Allan arrived on Friday evening she would still be looking into his eyes, Abby thought, but now she'd be squaring her shoulders and telling him as diplomatically as possible that she had changed her mind. There was no other choice. As much as she continued to believe he would make an excellent family man, she couldn't marry him.

The blunt truth, she knew, was that she couldn't marry anyone—not Allan or any other man, not as long as she felt far more than it was surely wise to feel for Ryan Larabee.

"PLANS FOR the rodeo dance are shaping up nicely," Abby's godmother told her companions on Friday over a noonday meal of thick ham sandwiches and creamy potato salad, both of which she'd fixed while

Ryan helped her husband with yet another chore that needed some additional muscle to accomplish.

It had become almost a weekday morning routine, Ryan thought as he sat in a bright corner of the Stockton kitchen. First a session with Lively, then giving Bill a hand around the ranch and getting some additional exercise that worked a few of the kinks out of a body being regularly rattled to the bone by his bull-riding efforts.

Today Gail had issued the invitation to join the couple for lunch when she'd returned from another committee meeting. He'd readily accepted. Besides having worked up an appetite, he enjoyed their company, Ryan had to admit. Somehow they treated him as family when he really wasn't family. *We consider you one of us,* he recalled Gail saying shortly after his arrival. It seemed they actually did.

"Can't wait to waltz my bride around in the Texas two-step," Bill told his wife, aiming a glance at her down the length of their farmhouse-style table.

"This year's band should know how to play a fine one," she replied. "I don't suppose they're called the Roughriders of the Stage for nothing."

"So it's a country-western theme?" Ryan ventured.

Gail nodded. "The gymnasium in the community center next to city hall is going to look as close to an old-time, frontier honky-tonk as we can get it, trust me."

"Barmaids and all," Bill said on a gusty sigh.

"What he means," Gail remarked dryly to Ryan, "is that he can't wait to get a long look at some of the younger women wearing costumes that are basically authentic—which means more than a little revealing.''

Ryan swallowed a bite of his sandwich and lifted a brow. "I take it this is an adult event."

"You're right on that score," the other man agreed with a distinct hint of devilment in his gaze, suddenly looking like someone who could have well-earned the title *Wild Bill*.

"The parade on Saturday morning will be geared for families," Gail explained. "We'll have rodeo clowns, along with the high-school marching band and a group of cowboys riding their horses, among other things—" she launched a meaningful glance at her husband "—but no barmaids to be ogled by men old enough to be their fathers."

"Now, honeybun—" Bill began.

"As long as you only look," Gail interrupted smoothly, "I won't have to resort to extreme measures."

"And what would those be?" Ryan inquired, earning himself a don't-egg-her-on narrowing of Bill's eyes.

Gail set her empty plate aside, having finished the smaller portions she'd taken in contrast to the men's heaping helpings, and placed her elbows on the table. "Let's just say that a smart man wouldn't want to find out."

"You're scaring me," Bill muttered. Then the pure devilment in his gaze was back full force as he smiled a long, slow smile.

"Okay, you're too tough to be scared," Gail allowed, propping her chin on an upraised fist, "but don't be too smug about it. I still plan on putting you to work again after lunch helping me paint the hallway trim.'' She glanced around the newly decorated kitchen. ''Things,'' she declared with satisfaction, ''are going well.''

''You bet.'' Bill aimed a brief look of his own over the long room bordering the rear of the house. Done mainly in earth tones, it was rustic enough to fit in with a more rugged setting, yet plainly comfortable, as well. ''This place is gonna look like a regular palace any day now,'' he contended, and joined his wife in another smile over that statement.

Knowing full well how pleased the couple was at the progress being made at the ranch, Ryan also recognized that his own mood had recently taken a turn for the better, undeniably helped along by the fact that he'd managed to make it to seven seconds twice that morning before Lively had sent him sprawling. He was making progress there, and it felt good, he had to admit.

So what if his ex-wife's fiancé was due to arrive that evening? If he could tackle a stubborn bull and make headway, he could handle the good doctor's visit, too. At least he could rein in his baser male instincts enough not to growl at the guy. Damn right he could, he assured himself as he forked up another mouthful of potato salad.

Just then the wall phone set at one side of a narrow window rang. ''I'll get it,'' Gail offered, pushing back from the table. She rose, smoothed a hand down the cotton dress she'd worn for the committee meeting and walked over to answer. ''Yes, he's here,'' she told the caller after a short beat. ''Tom Kennedy for you, Bill,'' she said, setting the receiver on the counter. ''I'm going to change into my painting clothes. Being the tough guy you are,'' she added archly, tossing the words over one shoulder as she left the kitchen, "you should have no trouble dealing with the dirty dishes."

A mock grimace crossed Bill's face. "I suppose a man's gotta do what a man's gotta do," he grumbled halfheartedly. Getting up, he took the police chief's call and lapsed into silence after a brief greeting.

Ryan finished the last of his sandwich and settled back in his chair, already having noted that the phone conversation was mainly one-sided. From all indications it was hardly the most cheerful, either, especially given that two old friends were involved.

"Okay, thanks," Bill said at last. "Larabee's with me now. I'll bring him up-to-date and tell him you'd like to see him. I expect he'll be stopping by your office shortly." With that, he hung up.

"You don't exactly look happy," Ryan pointed out as the older man returned to the table and sat down again. "I assume that was about the major."

"It was," Bill agreed, his quiet tone as sober as his expression. "We've got what you might say is a very interesting development."

Ryan leaned forward, his attention focused on the matter at hand. "Interesting?"

"Uh-huh. According to Tom, everything about the man checks out, including the fact that he was born in Virginia and served in many parts of the world during a long and distinguished military career before returning to his home state when he retired. It all fits…except for one thing."

"Which is?" Ryan prompted.

Bill's gaze met his. "Major Calvin Hobbs died six months ago after a short illness."

RYAN DRUMMED a finger on the smooth leather steering wheel as he drove back to Aunt Abigail's. A glance in his rearview mirror found Tom Kennedy and a uniformed policeman following in an official department car. The chief, pursuing his better-to-be-safe-than-sorry advice, was as eager as Ryan to talk to the bogus major. "Low-key" was how he had suggested they approach it during Ryan's brief stop at police headquarters. Just a few pertinent questions for a start, Tom had advised, and see where that led.

Ryan had warned the chief not to expect to be able to ask anything immediately, explaining that the major often spent his afternoons away from the bed and breakfast. With that fact in mind, Ryan was hardly surprised to see no sign of the major's midsize gray import when he pulled into the small paved lot next to the colorful flower garden bordering one side of the house.

Tom rolled down his window when Ryan walked over to tell him the major was out. The chief took the delay in stride. "I'll have Bert," he said, referring to his companion, "park a ways up the street and keep an eye on things from there. Whoever this guy turns out to be, I don't want a police car spooking him when he shows up. Meantime, we can wait inside."

Both men tugged their wide-brimmed hats down on their foreheads as they headed up the curving sidewalk, the same pathway lined with low bushes that Ryan had walked for the first time only weeks earlier, never expecting to learn so much about his own past from the people he would meet in Harmony. From all he'd been told about himself, Ryan reflected, he doubted he'd been someone who believed in fate, in things that were meant to be. Even now, he couldn't say he did, not really. But he had to wonder.

What if he had stayed holed up in his apartment down south, alone and staring at the walls? What then? He quickly discovered it was a prospect he'd rather not consider, and he let it go, deeming it better to keep his mind on the task at hand.

They found Ethel in the spacious living room, waving a plump feather duster over a mahogany coffee table. Painted roses decorated the oval table top, echoing those on the old-fashioned camelback sofa and spilling across the thick fringed rug covering much of the hardwood floor. Lacy white doilies on two bow-legged lamp tables matched both the curtains framing the tall front windows and the spotless apron worn by Everyone's Favorite Grandmother.

She aimed a welcoming smile at the men standing in the wide arched doorway. "Just what I like to see—a couple of strapping males who know how to do justice to a good meal. Which brings up the thought that I'm glad you stopped by, Tom. I've got two meatloaves in the refrigerator ready to pop into the oven, and you're welcome to come back for dinner—or take at least half a loaf home with you, if you want to bake it yourself. We have more than enough to go round. Abby's fiancé was going to join us, but he called a while ago to say he'd be a bit late tonight and not to hold dinner for him."

"Thanks, Ethel," Tom replied in his soft drawl as he ambled into the room and perched on the edge of a red-and-white striped wingback chair. "You know how to make an old bachelor's day. I'll take a hunk of that meatloaf with me if you don't mind, seeing as I've got a date with a baseball game on TV tonight."

"I understand. I'm a football fan, myself, you know."

First rock and roll, now football? That thought had Ryan shaking his head as he leaned one shoulder against the doorjamb and folded his arms over the twin front pockets of his denim shirt. "I noticed Major Hobbs's car is gone," he said, switching subjects and keeping his tone as casual as possible. "Any idea when he'll be back?"

Ethel's smile faded as she issued a regretful sigh. "I'm sorry to say he won't be."

Ryan frowned, wondering what that meant. Then he was afraid he knew. Unless he missed his guess, this was going to be another interesting development.

"He won't be back?" Tom asked carefully.

"No. Some sort of family emergency came up." Ethel abandoned her dusting and sank down on the sofa. "The dear man checked out late this morning."

Hell, was all Ryan could think, recognizing that a chance had been lost. And by just a few measly hours. "I'm not so sure how dear he was," he replied dryly, deciding there was no longer any point in mincing words. "The smooth-talking Major Hobbs seems to have been a total fake."

Abby arrived just in time to catch that last statement. It startled her for an instant before she took the last few steps that put her at Ryan's side. "A fake?" she repeated.

"And maybe a crook, as well," he told her.

"Goodness gracious, it couldn't be," Ethel said.

But it probably was, Abby had to concede after she joined the other woman on the sofa and Ryan's account of his vague suspicions was followed by the concrete facts the police chief had discovered. She could have asked why the far-too-attractive male still propped in the doorway with his black Stetson cocked at a rakish angle hadn't mentioned anything to her—indeed, she would have if she didn't know quite well that she'd gone out of her way to avoid any private conversations, both before and after the eventful day at the park.

Thankfully Cara, now napping peacefully upstairs, had emerged from the experience as healthy as ever, and Abby could only continue to be grateful for the part Ryan had played in the outcome. Nevertheless, she hadn't been able to ignore her own sense of caution that urged her to maintain some distance between them.

"Whoever the man actually was," Tom said, "if his departure had anything to do with the questions I asked in certain circles, he must have been a pretty sharp customer, because I did it as quietly as possible."

"He was at least sharp enough to get his hands on some very real-looking identification," Abby confessed, "because he actually showed me a Virginia driver's license with his picture on it so I could copy the number in the guest register along with the home address and phone number he gave me."

Tom absorbed that information and kept his gaze on Abby. "How did he pay for the room?"

"In cash—and by the week." She gave her head a wry shake. "In fact, I wound up giving him a refund when he left. He was paid up through Sunday."

"All nice and simple," Tom murmured with a considering expression.

"And untraceable," Ryan added.

"I know his car was a rental," Ethel said, "and I

believe he picked it up in Phoenix. I remember him telling me that while he enjoyed his drive here and it wasn't all that long, we might draw even more weekend visitors to Harmony if we had some sort of commuter air service.''

Tom nodded. ''I can try to follow up with the rental outfits, but the fact is, whatever the man might have been up to, we've probably seen the last of him.''

''For which we should no doubt be thankful,'' Abby said, releasing a short breath.

Tom lifted one shoulder in a shrug. ''Can't say I'd argue with that. I've got to admit I'd feel easier about the whole thing, though, if I knew why he came here in the first place.'' The chief paused for a beat, then asked, ''Did he call ahead from somewhere to make a reservation?''

''No,'' Abby replied after a moment, thinking back. ''He just appeared out of the blue one day, every inch a dapper Southern gentleman, and asked if there were any rooms available.''

''Which isn't all that unusual,'' Ethel pointed out. ''Sometimes people do drive by and like the look of the place.''

Abby leaned back in her seat and slanted a glance at the woman beside her. ''But isn't it true that the majority of guests call ahead, exactly as—'' She halted as a thought struck her.

''Exactly as what, dear?'' Ethel asked.

''As someone else did,'' she finished slowly. She redirected her gaze toward the doorway and the man still standing there. ''This may mean nothing, but it just occurred to me that the major showed up shortly after another guest's arrival. And when that guest stayed, he stayed, too.''

"Do you mean...?" Ethel left the question hanging.

Ryan's attention remained on Abby. "Yes," he replied with a thoughtful look. "She means me."

ABBY SAT on a low stone bench in the front yard, wishing Allan would get there. Throughout a dinner she'd done her best to eat, followed by the nightly routine of bathing Cara and then reading a children's story before the baby's early bedtime, a nagging question had remained foremost in her mind.

How do you break it to a man that you want to break it off? Especially when that man was someone you admired and dearly wanted to retain as a friend? A man you knew deserved more than you could give, and one bound to be snatched up by some lucky woman? A man who was dependable to the core, even if his recent behavior had proved to be somewhat of a puzzle?

She'd certainly been puzzled by the call she'd placed to Allan's office yesterday morning, Abby thought. A brief conversation just to touch base and confirm his visit was what she'd intended, given that he'd been out of town at his seminar the weekend before and they hadn't talked since his return. The call had turned out to be even briefer than she'd planned, however, when he'd suddenly brought it to a close, explaining it was a busy day. Which may well have been the case, she had to concede. Nonetheless, he hadn't sounded quite like himself, and she'd been wondering ever since whether something in her tone had conveyed more than she'd meant to over the phone.

Even more puzzling was his unexpected call

shortly after lunch today while she was out in the backyard with Cara, when he'd left a hasty message with Ethel to say he'd be late arriving this evening without offering any further explanation.

And it was definitely late, Abby reflected, glancing up at a moonlit sky. Still, those phone calls aside, Allan remained a solidly responsible person, and she had no doubt that if he said he would be here, he would. So she would continue to wait here until his car pulled in, ask him to join her for a short walk on this pleasantly cool night in order to allow them some time alone, then say what she had to say as tactfully as she could. After which she would take up her hostess duties, offer food and drink, and invite him to spend the night—or the rest of the weekend, as he'd originally planned—at Aunt Abigail's.

She had to hope he wouldn't be too upset, that he would accept her suggestion to stay here and give them the chance to spend more time together, not as an engaged couple, but as friends. At least, knowing Allan, she had reason to be optimistic. He wasn't, after all, a highly emotional person, and although he might be hurt, he also might well come to accept her decision as one that was ultimately best for both of them.

Yes, she had to hope for that.

Just then a car pulled in. Not Allan's, Abby noted, glancing at the well-lit lot. Four couples had checked in that afternoon for weekend stays. Two had already arrived back from dinner; this was the third. She waved a hello as they walked up the sidewalk to the front door.

Unfortunately their entry into the house coincided with the sight of the last person she wanted to see at that moment walking out. He wore his faded blue jacket over his jeans, a sign that he meant to stay outside for a while. Abby resisted the urge to sigh when he spotted her and started across the lawn.

"Mind if I sit down for a minute?" Ryan asked. With the bench set under a tall, old-style lantern lamp, she had no difficulty making out his expression as he gazed down at her. He didn't, she thought, look happy.

"I'm waiting for Allan," she said pointedly, folding her arms under breasts covered by a camel-colored pullover sweater.

He dipped his head in a nod that sent the light gleaming off his dark hair. "Figured you were. I promise to make myself scarce once he gets here."

"Okay," she agreed after a short hesitation. At least talking might take her mind off this endless waiting.

He sat down, leaving a good space between them. An owl hooted somewhere in the distance before he spoke. "I've been mulling over what you said earlier about the bogus major maybe following in my tracks."

So that's what was bothering him. "I could be wrong," she acknowledged. "His showing up when he did may have just been a coincidence." She paused, staring ahead into the darkness. "But the timing fits."

"It does," he allowed.

She slanted a sidelong glance his way. "Then again, why would he be interested in you?"

Ryan's brows drew together in a frown. "There's only one halfway sensible reason I've been able to come up with."

Frowning herself when he stopped at that point, Abby said, "What is it?"

"He was keeping tabs on me to see if my memory came back."

That won her attention in a hurry. She turned to fully face him. "If you're serious, and it certainly seems as though you are, do you think he's someone you've met in the past?"

"Could be. Although if I did know him from somewhere, it's tough to see why a guy we've discovered is hardly an upstanding citizen would risk jogging my memory."

Abby's frown deepened. "But if it wasn't him personally he may have been concerned about you remembering, what was it?"

A silent moment passed before Ryan blew out a breath. "It could have something to do with the last weekend in May."

"What?"

"I think something, not in Harmony but maybe down south, is scheduled to happen then." And with those words, Ryan went on to offer an explanation that had Abby staring. "Trouble is," he summed up minutes later, "I've got nothing more to go on than the fact that it might have something to do with the lounge I was seen leaving the night before I crashed."

"And your colleague didn't recognize anyone there when he walked in after you left," Abby said, attempting to get what she'd just been told straight in her mind.

"Uh-uh." He slapped a hand on his knee. "And the devil of it is, that place may have zip to do with it."

Abby couldn't disagree. "That's true," she said,

"but then maybe you weren't followed here, either. And maybe whatever might be happening at the end of May isn't anything terrible."

Ryan's mouth curved in a thin smile. "Are you trying to tell me to look on the bright side?"

She shrugged. "I suppose so. After all—"

"Hello, Abby," a familiar voice said, breaking in. Allan. She'd been so engrossed in the current conversation that she hadn't even noticed his car pulling in. Mentally squaring her shoulders, Abby turned her gaze to the man standing steps away. Then her eyes went wide and she surged to her feet.

"My God, Allan, were you in an accident?" It was the first thought to hit at the sight of a man who bore little resemblance to the calmly competent professional so familiar to her—a man who currently looked as if a small tornado had picked him up and dropped him in the front yard.

"No," he said, holding up a restraining palm before she could take a step toward him. "I haven't been in an accident. Really, I'm…fine."

Fine? Abby ran her gaze again over a well-tailored yet sadly rumpled gray suit. Not only were Allan's clothes never rumpled, his designer silk ties never looked as though they'd come out of a blender. And his hair—his expertly cut, strikingly gold hair—was never the least bit disordered, much less thoroughly mussed as it was now.

"You can't," Abby told him, "be fine."

"I think this is my cue to leave," Ryan slid in.

Again Allan held up a restraining hand. "No, don't go," he said as if he didn't relish being left alone with his fiancée. He let out a long breath. "I mean, feel free to stay."

Remaining seated, Ryan warned, "You might not think that's such a good idea when you find out who I am."

The statement stopped Allan cold for a second. "You, ah, must be Abby's former husband."

"I must be," Ryan said dryly. "Should I take off now?"

Allan shook his head. "It still might be better if you stayed."

"Abby?" Ryan questioned.

She slowly sat back down. "I guess," she said, keeping her gaze on Allan, "it wouldn't hurt if you stayed for a minute."

"Any idea what this is all about?" Ryan asked her, dropping his voice to a low murmur.

"Not a clue," she replied out of the corner of her mouth before raising her voice again. "Allan, this is Ryan Larabee," she said by way of introduction, hoping under the circumstances that no one would find it necessary to shake hands.

No one did. Instead Allan lifted a hand and raked it through his hair, which only mussed it more. "It's hard to believe," he said, casting a rueful glance down at himself, "that this all started with a pair of purple shoes."

Abby found herself speechless. "Purple shoes?" she finally ventured carefully.

"Yes. Bright purple, in fact." Allan widened his stance and put his fists on his hips. "Grace bought them last week."

"Grace?" Ryan muttered, again dropping his voice.

"His nurse and office assistant," Abby explained under her breath. His oh-so-conventional assistant, she could have added, and the last woman she would have expected to buy shoes in what was by no stretch of the imagination a conservative color.

"I mean *purple*," Allan went on, as though his thoughts matched hers. "Plus they weren't even real shoes—more like sandals, with little straps and thin heels high enough to be totally impractical. And to top it all off, she started wearing them to the office every day. It was," he declared, "amazing."

Abby could well believe it. Grace of the wire-rimmed glasses, scraped-back hair and makeup-free face abandoning her sensible white oxfords for a far different mode of footwear would be a sight sure to raise eyebrows. Especially Allan's.

"And the thing was," he said, continuing, "I couldn't stop looking at them. Or thinking about them. Last week I was attending a major seminar on child development that deserved my full attention, but I kept wondering about those shoes. Why in the world did Grace buy them? I kept asking myself. Then when I got back to the office on Monday, she had a new hairdo, too. Something short and curly and frivolous. Plus she had lipstick on—bright pink lipstick. I didn't like it. It wasn't Grace!"

Not the Grace you saw only in one light, Abby reflected with assurance. Not the woman you viewed as a nurturing, motherly type despite her being just a few years older than you. Well, hooray for her, Abby thought. It was time Allan's eyes were opened to a few things, even if the truth of that wasn't helping him now.

"I'm sorry you're upset," she offered calmly, "but—"

"But that wasn't the end of it," he said, forging

on. "Late yesterday, after the last patient was taken care of, I was in my office writing up some reports when Grace walked in, still wearing those purple shoes." He paused. "Only this time she wasn't wearing anything else."

"Whoa." Ryan cleared his throat. "Sorry."

"No, I'm the one who's sorry," Allan countered. "Not for what happened next, I'll admit, because it was as though it was meant to be, as though I had to make love to her then and there. We made love all night, in fact. In the *office*. Neither of us seemed to be able to get enough."

Allan? Wildly passionate? Abby was still absorbing that startling piece of information when he again forged on.

"I haven't slept in who knows how long. I look like I've been dragged through a keyhole. And I can't regret any of it—even though I do regret something." His handsome features settled into sober lines. "What I am truly and deeply sorry for is that I wasn't thinking about anyone else's feelings at the time. I know you probably wouldn't have me on a silver platter after what I've just told you, Abby. Yet even if by some miracle you would, I couldn't go through with it. I admire you more than I can say and always will. But I can't marry you."

Chapter Eight

Ryan directed a probing glance at the woman seated beside him and found her expression frozen fast, as still and stiff as the stone bench under them. Probably in a state of shock, he concluded. Which was hardly surprising. He'd been thrown for a loop himself.

And after stark seconds ticked by, he also had to admit to being thankful when Abby drew in a measured breath and regained her voice. "I understand, Allan," she said, her even tone no more revealing than her expression.

"Do you really?" the man still standing steps away asked, his solemn expression rigidly in place.

She lowered her chin in the briefest of nods. "Yes. I wish you and Grace the best."

At that statement, his broad shoulders slumped slightly in clear relief. "Thank you, Abby. I'll tell Grace. I'm crazy about her," he confessed after a beat, shaking his head with what might have been wonder. "Or maybe I'm just crazy, but I can't give her up."

Abby smiled a little. Bravely, Ryan thought. "Be happy," she said.

The doctor walked forward then and Ryan took it

as his signal to give them some space. Not that he was leaving Abby alone to deal with this, but some things deserved privacy. At least a sensitive man would think so, he told himself as he moved out of listening range.

Whatever he did, he would not jump for joy at the end of his ex-wife's engagement. A part of him might want to, but he damn well wouldn't, not any more than he would give in to another part that urged him to plant a fist on Dr. Wonderful's chiseled jaw for hurting Abby.

With the latter resolve firmly in mind, Ryan jammed his hands into his pockets when Allan approached him with quick strides moments later.

"Wish I could say it was a pleasure meeting you, Larabee," Allan said with a rueful curve of his lips, "but I don't imagine anyone got much pleasure out of the past few minutes."

Ryan set his teeth. "Right."

The doctor looked at him. "I don't know what went wrong between you and Abby, but I do genuinely hope you'll both find your own particular happiness." And with those earnest words he continued on his way to the parking lot.

Cripes, now he couldn't even be mad at the guy. Or maybe he could, Ryan decided when he saw Abby bent over in her seat with her face in her hands.

Had his gut always twisted at the sight of a woman grieving? It seemed natural enough to have him thinking that maybe he hadn't been quite the self-centered SOB he'd learned he might be.

He sat down beside her, wondering what to do next. "Uh, Abby..."

"Has he gone?" she asked, her tone muffled.

"Yeah." Ryan reached up and rubbed the back of his neck. "But I can always haul him back here and kick his butt, if it'll make you feel better."

"That won't be necessary," she said.

To Ryan's ears, the words came out strained, as though she were trying to hold herself in check. "You don't have to be brave anymore," he told her as gently as he could. "You can bawl like a baby if you want to."

But she didn't bawl, like a baby or otherwise. Instead, still bent over, she dropped her hands and began to laugh. And laugh.

Not hysterically, though, Ryan was quick to note as he leaned in for a closer look. No, she was simply having a whopping good time. He flat-out couldn't believe it.

"What the devil is going on?" He had to raise his voice to a low roar in order to make himself heard as she continued to laugh...and laugh.

Finally she stopped long enough to wail, "The irony of it is just too funny. I was going to dump him—and instead he dumped me!"

And then the unbridled humor took over again while Ryan stared at her with his mouth open. "You were going to dump *him?*"

She nodded and brushed tears of pure amusement from her cheeks. "I was. In fact, I had myself tied up in knots trying to decide how to do it so he wouldn't be too hurt." She drew in a lengthy breath and gradually released it. "And then he turned the tables before I could even begin to tell him that I couldn't marry him."

Ryan voiced the first question that popped into his head. "Why couldn't you marry him?"

That had her changing gears in a hurry. Abby straightened and stared straight ahead, all traces of humor gone. "Because."

He frowned. "That's not exactly an answer. Want to give it another try?"

She turned her head, little by little, and studied him for a long moment, as though trying to decide whether to say anything more. He'd nearly concluded that she'd chosen not to when she spoke at last, her voice quiet yet clear in the silence all around them. "I couldn't marry him because I discovered that I still feel too much for someone else."

Ryan froze. He didn't have to ask who that someone was. Her steady gaze, candid even in the muted light, told him as plainly as if she'd shouted it. Willing his muscles to move, he reached up and brushed a last tear from her cheek, felt the smoothness of her skin under his fingers and knew he would never be satisfied until he'd touched every inch of her.

"Do you want him?" he asked, leaning closer still. "I hope to heaven you do," he added in the next breath, "because he sure as blazes wants you."

One second stretched to five before she issued words that sent his pulse rate soaring. "Yes," she said simply, "I want him."

"Glory be," he murmured as his arms locked around her. And then his mouth came down on hers in a deep, hard kiss, a swift melding of lips and tastes. Far from tentative, it was a kiss that left no room for indecision, only mounting needs to be met and rising tension to be eased. Much to Ryan's regret, it was also a kiss that didn't last nearly long enough to suit him before Abby pulled away.

''We're in the front yard,'' she reminded him on a breathless gasp. ''Anyone could walk by.''

And, as if to prove her point, the sound of soft footsteps had them both wrenching around to look forward as a couple holding hands, both dressed casually in sweaters and jeans, came ambling down the sidewalk from the direction of the parking lot. Ryan recognized them as more of Aunt Abigail's guests. He'd met them briefly in the hall earlier, and now he wished them anywhere but where they were.

''Maybe they won't notice us,'' he told Abby, keeping his voice low. ''Maybe they'll just go inside and go to bed.''

Which was exactly where he wanted to go, and not alone. But not just any bed partner would fill the bill, he knew. Only one particular woman would do.

That woman quietly slid to one side, putting a short space between them. ''They're the last of the guests to come back from dinner,'' she informed him in a whisper. ''I can lock up for the night after they go in.''

''And then we can go upstairs and pick up where we left off,'' Ryan finished, slanting a meaningful look her way.

''Yes,'' she replied after a silent second, gazing straight into his eyes.

He resisted the urge to throw up a tight fist and shout in sheer male triumph. Barely. Unfortunately, the new arrivals noticed them anyway. Smiling, they picked their way across the grassy lawn to the bench. ''Nice night,'' the light-haired, thirty-something man said.

''Yes,'' Abby replied.

''A little on the chilly side now, don't you think?''

Ryan offered as blandly as he could. "A good night for sleeping." To reinforce his point, he yawned into his hand.

"Oh, it would be a shame to let that sky full of stars go to waste," the blond female half of the All-American couple protested lightly.

"In that case," Abby said after a brief hesitation, "you're welcome to use the bench if you want to sit out for a while." Her tone was staunchly gracious, even if not precisely enthusiastic.

"Well, maybe for a few min—" the man started to say.

"Speaking of sleeping, the feather beds here are very comfy, don't you think?" Ryan asked, breaking in and hoping he'd done it easily enough not to make it too noticeable. "I'm assuming you were lucky enough to get a room with one. If you didn't, it would be a shame."

The shift in subjects seemed to bring the other man up short. "Actually we do have one, but we, uh, haven't tried ours yet. It'll be a new experience."

Ryan arched an eyebrow and launched a deliberately male-to-male look. "I think you'll find it...pleasurable."

Clean-cut type or not, the guy clearly recognized the possibilities in that statement. His own brows took a quick hike. "Really?"

"Definitely."

"Maybe it is getting a bit cold out," the man said, switching his attention to his partner.

Abby directed her own that-was-quite-a-snow-job look at Ryan as he rose and pulled her up beside him, catching her hand in his. "Why don't we all go in?" he suggested. "The weather's going to be great tomorrow. We can get a good night's rest and be up early to enjoy it.''

When the couple merely nodded in response and headed toward the house, Ryan held Abby back for a second. "I'll make sure everything's locked up," he said, then paused for a quiet beat. "Your room or mine?"

She gazed up at him, eyes gleaming in the darkness. "Mine. Since Cara's in the adjoining room, I can leave the door open a crack to hear her if she needs me."

"Okay." He released her hand. "Go on in."

She hesitated. "Aren't you coming?"

"I need a little more cold air to settle me down," he told her frankly, "but I'll be upstairs shortly and knocking on your door." His smile was slow and wide. "Then I promise to warm both of us up."

SHE WAS ALREADY WARM, Abby thought as she slipped her silky green nightgown over her head. And not as calm as she would have liked, she couldn't deny. Although under the circumstances, she supposed that was to be expected. After all, it wasn't every day a woman lost a fiancé and acquired a lover who just happened to be her ex-husband. The situation was, in a word, *unique.*

It was also playing havoc with her nerves.

Nevertheless, she wasn't sorry for having given in to the impulse to tell Ryan how she felt and agreeing to welcome him to her room. Maybe regrets, plenty of them, would surface tomorrow. She was well aware that the practical person she'd become over the course of the last several years seldom acted rashly.

So the voice of reason might well berate her for doing something wildly foolish when the sun rose.

But not tonight.

Tonight she wasn't questioning the wisdom of the choices she'd made. In fact, the only question she would allow herself at the moment was whether to climb into bed or stay where she was until her visitor arrived.

"Hardly an earthshaking decision," she told her reflection in the mirror topping a whitewashed oak dresser that matched the simple, stylish lines of the rest of the room's furnishings. "And not that it matters much one way or the other," she added, "because if I'm not in bed when he gets here, I'm sure to be soon after."

Prior experience, although by no means recent, had her certain of her words. The man she'd known so intimately had been more than ready to slip between the sheets with dispatch. It was true that, once there, a fast-and-furious approach hadn't been foremost in his mind on every occasion. He had readily given her time to catch up when she'd needed it. But, as with so many things in his life in those days, a speedy rush to pleasure had plainly been to his liking.

Mutual pleasure, to be sure. Even though he hadn't turned out to be perfect husband material, Ryan Larabee had been a generous lover, and a faithful one, as well. Abby could scarcely contend otherwise. Women had always found him attractive, but she'd never doubted that while she was his wife, she'd been the only woman he carried off to bed and...

"And why am I indulging in mental trips down memory lane when I should be deciding what to do next?" she asked, reining in her thoughts. Her image, muted in the single small light she'd left on by the queen-size bed, didn't appear to have an answer for that one.

Then a quiet knock sounded and she knew the time for decision had passed. ''Come in,'' she called softly as she turned from the mirror.

He came in, wearing a pair of jeans and nothing else. Her toes curled in the thick carpet at the sight. She had seen him dressed in even less countless times, of course. Still, she couldn't recall ever being able to take the prospect of having the whole length of him on full view for granted. Certainly she couldn't do it now.

No, definitely not now.

''Hi,'' he said, his voice low and husky. Turning quickly, he closed the door and locked it, then started toward her with silent, steady steps.

She squared shoulders covered only by the thin straps of her ankle-length gown and tried for a light tone. ''Hi, yourself.'' Despite her efforts, the words came out far less breezy than she'd intended.

Holding her gaze with his own, he stopped scarcely inches away and reached out to run his hands up her bare arms. His palms were rough, his touch tender. The contrast and the thoroughness of the gesture as he repeated it for good measure had a familiar shiver sliding down her spine.

So much, she thought with an inward sigh, for being casual about this.

As though well aware of her reaction, Ryan smiled a small, satisfied smile, one that slowly faded as he bent his head to bring his lips to hers. This time, his kiss was as thorough as his touch, one of intimate promise rather than swift and stark desire.

And this time, it was he who ended it by gently pulling back, somewhat to her surprise.

"Are we, ah, going to bed?" she asked in a whisper against his mouth.

"How about if we try something else first?" he countered, and with that he picked her up in one sweeping motion and carried her to a high-backed armchair beside the nightstand. There, he sat down and settled her in his lap.

Things, she realized, were not going exactly the way she'd imagined. Then again, given the circumstances, this was probably one of those occasions when she would need time to catch up, so proceeding full speed ahead wasn't precisely to her benefit. The problem was, she was far from sure how successful she'd be at marshalling her wits enough to keep up her end of a conversation, if that's what the man who held her in a light grasp had in mind.

"Comfortable?" he asked, again meeting her gaze. With her yielding bottom perched on his rock-solid thighs, they were nearly eye-to-eye.

"Mmm-hmm," she murmured, assuming he meant literally. On another level, of course, she was anything but comfortable. And she might as well come clean in that regard, she told herself. "I have to admit I'm a little nervous."

"There's no reason to be," he replied mildly, resting his head on the back of the chair. "When you think about it, I'm the one who should be nervous."

That statement had her blinking, since she'd never known him to be the least bit shy when it came to physical intimacy. Far from it. "You?"

He nodded. "This is all new to me, you could say, because I can't remember ever making love before."

Eyes widening, she sat up straight and stared, her nerves forgotten. "Good grief, I never considered that aspect of it."

"Me, neither," he confessed. "Not until the thought hit as I crossed the hall to knock on your door, at any rate." He paused, reaching up to tuck a strand of her newly brushed hair behind her ear. "I guess you'll just have to teach me."

Teach him? *Him?*

The man she more than suspected had been well on his way to becoming an expert soon after puberty? The undeniably attractive male who, even minus his memory, seemed to have little trouble sparking a thoroughly feminine response? "You didn't need any help when it came to kissing," she reminded him, recalling several recent incidents.

"Maybe not," he allowed, pulling her closer in a slow and steady motion, "but the rest of it is bound to be a tad more…complicated."

Complicated. The word suddenly held a wealth of meaning. "I suppose so," she agreed as the beginnings of another shiver surfaced.

"If you want to get it right, that is." His brilliant blue gaze took on a purposeful gleam. "And I definitely want to get it right."

She ran her tongue over her lips. "Right," she had to concede, "would be good."

"All things considered," he summed up, "I think at least a few pointers are in order."

"So you're asking me to—" Abby released a short breath "—show you."

"If you don't mind."

"No, I guess I don't," she said after a thoughtful moment, discovering that was actually true. The idea of a major role reversal intrigued her. In the past he had been the far-more-experienced partner. Now she had the chance to take the lead. "This," she declared, smiling a genuinely enthusiastic smile, "could turn out to be very interesting."

"I get the impression you're warming to the notion," he said with a twist of his lips. "Just take it easy on me."

But she didn't. Couldn't. Rather than holding back, she wrapped her arms around him and kissed him with everything she had, leaving them both gasping for air when it ended, then swiftly sent her lips on a downward journey over his neck and shoulders, relishing both the taste of him and the strength underlying his leanly muscled skin.

Before long, she had him out of the chair and out of his jeans, after which his hands proved to be equally adept at removing her nightgown.

"Glory be," Ryan muttered, looking his fill as they stood beside the bed. "You are one downright gorgeous sight."

"So," she didn't hesitate to reply, letting her eyes roam at will, "are you."

He drew in a ragged breath. "What comes next?"

She brushed a hand over his hair-darkened chest. "Touching. Lots of touching." And then, eagerly pursuing her instructor's role, she offered tips on how to touch her while she touched him, and wasn't much surprised when he came up with a few variations of his own. When her knees threatened to buckle, she suggested they lie down.

"Think I'm ready?" he asked, his lips at her ear as he kept her upright with a bolstering arm around her waist.

"You're more than ready, trust me," she informed him, fully mindful of some of the places she'd just investigated.

Ryan released her then and she sank down on the bed. Leaning over, she opened the top drawer of the nightstand and pulled out one of the foil packets she'd retrieved from a supply closet. Aunt Abigail's was touted to provide all the comforts of home, and that included protection discreetly placed in the cabinets of its graciously old-style bathrooms.

"I don't suppose you recall using anything like this," she said, glancing up at the man who was about to become her lover for the second time.

"Uh-uh." He sat beside her and, deftly performing his pupil's duties, stroked a palm over her breast in the very way she'd indicated she liked best. "You'll have to show me."

She did when they were stretched out side by side, and Ryan had to grit his teeth to stop a groan at the feel of her smooth fingers on him. He'd told Abby the total truth. He had no recollection of making love before. But that didn't stop the male core of him from responding, he thought, just as it had responded to one degree or another since he'd met a long-legged, flame-haired woman on his first day in Harmony. Tonight, however, it wouldn't be satisfied with merely looking. Or kissing. Or touching.

Tonight it wanted—he wanted—everything. All of her. And soon.

His natural inclination was to pull her under him, but she moved first and wiggled her way up and over. "I guess the teacher gets to be on top," he said, gazing up into the smoky-green eyes that had appeared in more than one of his midnight fantasies during the past weeks. He'd had to imagine certain other parts of her then. But no longer.

Now nothing barred the sight of her softly curved breasts, nipped-in waist and gently flared hips. Now he could see what the blank wall in his mind had denied him—everything, all of her. And he could only be thankful.

"The teacher also gets to set the pace," she told him, looking pleased with the situation. And that said, she brought them together, slowly and completely.

This time Ryan couldn't suppress a low, lengthy groan. It felt too damn good. Better than he'd known anything could feel. Better than he could even imagine anything feeling. In fact, it felt like sheer heaven.

Abby lifted a tawny eyebrow as she started to move. "Am I hurting you?"

"You're killing me." His hands fisted at his sides. "And whatever you do, don't stop."

A quiet laugh spilled out. "What kind of teacher would I be if I threw in the towel before the lesson's over?" And far from halting, she picked up the pace.

"Don't forget my gold star if I survive," he managed to get out in a near growl before speech deserted him.

Then they began to move in tandem as he gripped her hips and found the rhythm. His brain had to struggle to think, but the rest of him soared free. His body knew what to do, where it craved to go and how to get there.

But no part of him, as it turned out, wanted to get there alone.

Don't let go too soon, something told him as his thrusts came faster and faster. *The rewards will be greater if you stay with it. Wait,* it said. *Wait.*

And he did.

Untold minutes later the woman above him shuddered as they arrived at their destination together. Then she slumped forward to rest her head on his chest, and he held her as endless waves of release rolled through him.

He lost himself in it, and found true peace.

ABBY DRIFTED BACK to a sense of her surroundings. Even with her eyes shut tight, the sound of mingled breaths and the feel of crisp chest hair under her cheek had her fully conscious of the fact that making love with Ryan had been no dream. No, this was real, and so was he.

With her ear pressed against him, she could hear his heart still beating fast and knew her own hadn't yet slowed to normal. Or what had been normal when the moon rose in the sky hours earlier. Now she more than suspected that her concept of normal would never be quite the same.

Something, she thought, had changed.

She'd experienced a fundamental shift in her personal world before, when she and Ryan had gone their separate ways. Then, the change brought about by their divorce had rocked her to the core. This time, though, she felt on firmer footing, perhaps because she was older and wiser and no longer believed that happily-ever-afters were a given. This time, it seemed as if she could take another change in their relationship in stride, maybe enough to keep regrets at bay when the sun dawned.

Maybe, Abby reflected as her eyes fluttered open, she could do something she'd never truly done before: set thoughts of the future completely aside and simply appreciate the rewards of the present. A present that included Ryan Larabee. After all, the fact was that they had become lovers again, and however much that prospect would have won her total amazement only weeks earlier, it had happened.

Now, could she just enjoy it?

Abby sighed, thinking that at the moment it was far from difficult to take pleasure in the rugged body stretched out under her. No, not difficult at all, she concluded as she ran her fingers over skin turned to light bronze by the soft light. She drew in a long whiff of warm man, sighed again and snuggled closer.

"If you keep wiggling around," a low voice told her, "I'm going to be tempted to try for another gold star, and I don't think I'm up to it yet."

She lifted her head and peeked up at him. Strands of hair hung down his forehead, giving him a roguish air. His gaze was hooded, but she didn't miss the satisfied gleam in his eyes. Maybe, she decided, a little too satisfied.

With tongue firmly in cheek, she said, "Not up to it? Hmm, I guess you're not as young as you used to be."

He stared down at her and arched a brow. "You mean I didn't have any trouble...?"

"Not much," she supplied sweetly when he left the question hanging. Yes, she was definitely enjoying this.

"Hell." He blew out a gusty breath. "I know I'm on the far side of thirty, but I didn't figure on being over the hill this soon."

"Next thing you know," she said in the mildest of tones, "babies will start taking you for someone's grandfather."

He shot her a look that had her struggling to hold back a laugh.

"Remind me," he told her, "to get even with you later for that zinger. Right now, I suppose I have to take care of something in the bathroom."

"I believe you do." With that, she slid off him and pulled the white top sheet to her breasts, fully intending to enjoy herself even more by watching him depart. And she did, staring after him seconds later when he started for the door.

The rear view was as impressive as ever, she decided, before noting some dark bruises on a tight male backside. From his accident? she wondered. It hardly seemed likely after all this time. Even the long scar on his thigh wasn't all that noticeable. Unless he brought up the subject, though, his injuries were his business and none of hers, she reminded herself, still watching as he opened the door and started down the hall to the bath.

Thankfully, since they were the only ones occupying the family side of the second floor, and with the hallway door to the guest half of the house shut, no one would be complaining about naked men roaming around at midnight. Which it nearly was, Abby saw with a glance at the bedside clock. The lateness of the hour had her realizing that she had better get some sleep. She knew her little girl was sure to be up early, ready to eat breakfast.

Wrapping the sheet around herself, Abby got up and silently crossed the carpet to peek through the doorway into the adjoining room. As she'd expected, Cara was in dreamland, her dark lashes and rosy cheeks just visible in the glow of a nearby nightlight. At least one of them was getting a good night's rest,

Abby reflected with a fleeting smile as she drew the door toward her, leaving it open a crack.

After making her way back across the room, she straightened the satin bedspread in grave danger of falling to the floor, fluffed the pillows—not, fortunately for Ryan's allergy, of the down-filled variety—and had barely reclined again when he returned.

"Time to go to sleep," she told him, sliding over.

The words were scarcely out when he leaped into bed and pulled her under him. "I'm getting my second wind," he said as a sexy grin surfaced, displaying a row of wickedly gleaming teeth.

Startled at the sight, Abby could only stare. It was, she recognized full well, a stark flash of the old Ryan, the first she'd seen since they'd met after six long years. And it was as charmingly devastating as ever.

"I take it," she managed to get out, "that you don't need any more instruction."

If anything, his grin only widened. "I've discovered I'm a quick study," he murmured, bending to bring his lips to hers.

And then—skillfully, thoroughly and enthusiastically—he proceeded to demonstrate in no uncertain terms exactly how fast a learner he was.

Chapter Nine

"You look a little tired," Ethel told Abby as the older woman broke eggs into a large mixing bowl in preparation for making French toast, a featured item on Saturday's breakfast menu. "Did you get enough sleep, dear?"

Not hardly, Abby thought, swallowing a yawn as she leaned back in a kitchen chair. Still, although her eyelids might be in danger of drooping, other parts of her continued to hum right along in the aftermath of the pleasure she'd taken in Ryan's newly discovered skills. He deserved a gold star, she had to admit. Maybe a whole string of them.

"I probably didn't sleep as much as I should have," she acknowledged in a neutral tone.

At the counter, steps away, Ethel measured milk into the bowl, then sprinkled in sugar and dropped in a dash of vanilla. The yeasty scent of bread already baking in the oven filled the air. "I take it Allan didn't arrive until quite late," she said, bending to retrieve a wire whisk from the utensil drawer next to the stove. "Do you think he'll be down for breakfast soon?"

Abby knew she'd be facing this moment sooner or

later, and as far as she was concerned, sooner was better. In fact, she'd been waiting for the right opportunity to introduce the subject as she'd fed Cara, realizing that Ethel, having followed her usual habit of retiring to her room early to watch some favorite television programs, would have no clue as to the prior evening's surprising events. Now, with Cara investigating the contents of a low cabinet stocked with small kitchen items safe enough for baby's play, the chance had come to bring Ethel up to date.

"I'm afraid Allan won't be joining us for breakfast," Abby said. "He did get here fairly late, but he only stayed for a short while."

Ethel stopped blending the egg mixture and aimed a quick glance at Abby. "Is everything all right?"

"Yes," she replied, curving her lips in a reassuring smile. "Everything's fine, even though something has happened." She paused for a tick of the kitchen clock. "Allan and I are no longer engaged. I suppose the best way to put it is that we agreed to disagree. But we also agreed to remain friends." Thankfully that was true. They'd said their private goodbyes to each other with the promise to keep in touch. Which, she mused, might well be a telling indication of precisely how passionate their relationship had not been.

"You don't seem too upset about the breakup," Ethel said quietly after a silent second.

"I can't say that I am." Abby folded her arms across the front of another of her tailored blouses. "It was a mutual decision," she added, and left it at that.

"I see," Ethel murmured with a lifted brow before turning back to her task.

It didn't escape Abby's notice that the older woman seemed far from upset herself. She had to wonder how a full disclosure of last night's events would be received. Would Ethel be shocked? No, Abby didn't think so. Pleased? Maybe, she conceded after a thoughtful moment.

Ethel had certainly never been reluctant to reveal her liking for the man who had left Abby's bed early that morning—early enough that she'd still been fast asleep. Rather than finding his head lying next to hers when her eyes had opened at the cheerful sound of birds chirping outside her window, she'd discovered one of Aunt Abigail's special sugar-and-spice cookies wrapped in clear cellophane and tied with a delicate floral ribbon resting on the pillow.

He had probably, she thought now with a purse of her lips, snagged it from the empty guest room reserved for her ex-fiancé, which appeared to be a lot more likely than his raiding the well-stocked cookie jar in the downstairs pantry and wrapping it up himself. Whatever the case, though, she had no regrets about having savored every moist and tasty morsel before dragging herself out of bed.

The truth was, she had no regrets at all. As it turned out, none had surfaced with the inevitable dawn of a new day, which made her even more hopeful that she could put aside any questions about the future and simply enjoy the present.

A present that included Ryan Larabee.

Just then, as if her thoughts had summoned him, he ambled in from the hall dressed in jeans and a white T-shirt. If he'd even attempted to hold back a yawn, as she had earlier, he hadn't succeeded in foiling the one that had his mouth stretched wide for an instant before his gaze met hers.

''Sorry,'' he said in a slightly craggy voice, referring to the yawn and not by any means to what had happened between them. She knew that by the glint in his eyes fully visible across the room; a glint that displayed an utter lack of remorse even as it spoke volumes on the matter of pure masculine content. Not only wasn't he sorry, he was more than willing to do it all over again. Of that she was positive.

And since she was also fairly sure that he needed as much help keeping his eyes propped open as she did, it came as no surprise when he pulled his gaze away and wasted no time in heading for the coffee-maker.

Ethel slanted a glance at him and offered a bright greeting. "Good morning, Ryan."

"Morning," he replied in return as he poured himself a cup of dark brew.

"You look like you could use a bit more sleep," Ethel said. "Just as Abby does," she added after a thoughtful beat. "In fact, you both seem to be as tired as you were last Saturday morning. Only this time we didn't celebrate any birthdays," she pointed out in the lightest of tones.

It didn't fool Abby for a minute. Nor Ryan, judging by the way his gaze narrowed knowingly for a second as he leaned a hip against the counter. He took a long sip of his coffee, then matched Ethel's tone as he spoke. "No celebration," he agreed, "but I guess I did do some tossing and turning last night."

As in tossing the covers right off the bed to allow him plenty of room to reacquaint himself with every inch of her, Abby reflected with a flutter of her lashes. As in turning the light off only after they'd both given in to sheer and undeniably sweet exhaustion in the wee hours of the morning.

Ethel tilted her head. "Maybe you should have come down to the kitchen and fixed yourself a cup of warm milk," she said, studying him now. "It can help relax a person."

One corner of his mouth quirked up. "I have to admit that idea never crossed my mind. Good thing I managed to relax without it...eventually."

Suddenly the oven timer sounded, its low buzz drowning out the sputtered laugh Abby couldn't quite hide with a fake cough. Thankfully, by the time two fragrant bread loaves had been placed to cool on the counter, she had herself under control again.

Then it was Cara's turn to win everyone's notice as the baby slammed the cabinet shut, babbling as if to say, "I'm done with this." In the next breath she used the curved door handle to tug herself to a standing position.

Abby had to smile. "Maybe she'll decide to give walking another try today," she said. "I've tried to coax her into taking a few steps on her own ever since the day at the park, but she just stares at me, eyes wide, whenever I urge her on."

Which was exactly what the baby did now when Abby leaned forward, clapped her hands softly and held them out. "Come on, Cara, you can do it."

"I'm afraid she's not ready, dear," Ethel finally murmured.

"She sure looked ready when she made tracks for that lagoon," Ryan said.

And, as if the sound of his voice was all she needed to spur her on, Cara abruptly let go of the door and started toward him, her small body, dressed in cartoon-character pajamas, tottering as she let out a shout. "Pips!"

Ryan barely had time to drop to a crouch and catch her as she reached him. With his coffee cup still held in one hand, he wrapped his other arm lightly around her. "She's ready, all right," he announced with an I told-you-so glance up at Ethel.

"Yes, she certainly is," the older woman agreed, studying him again for a moment before returning to her breakfast preparations with the mildest of expressions.

But for the second time in minutes Abby wasn't fooled, fully conscious of the fact that, although Ryan might not realize it, he'd just been sized up as potential father material. Abby frowned, equally aware that speculation on that subject wasn't something she'd planned on. Or would encourage, she promised herself, watching as the baby spun around in Ryan's loose grip and took off again, this time straight toward her.

"Good girl," Abby said, her smile reappearing as she caught Cara close an instant later. Through the hand of fate, she thought, this child had become hers, and she would do everything in her power to be the best parent she could. Maybe the best single parent, if it turned out that she'd be raising Cara alone.

But whatever the future held, one thing she would not do was risk opening wounds long since healed by revisiting the past when it came to the topic of her former husband and fatherhood. Heaven knows, she and Ryan had discussed the matter before, years ago and at length. But that was then. This was now. And the last thing she wanted to do was talk about it.

The plain truth was, she no longer wanted to even think about it.

"TO MY WAY of looking at life, people are only as old as they convince themselves they are," Floyd Crenshaw—full-time barber and part-time philosopher—told Ryan later that morning. "I won't argue the fact that this shop dates back to my granddad's time, or that the equipment's been around since my dad's early days in the business. Truth is, I took over here when you were probably still wet behind the ears. But I don't for one minute consider myself old. No, sir."

Ryan viewed the tall and lanky man in the mirrored wall that had served as a backdrop for countless haircuts. When he'd mentioned the need to get one himself after breakfast, Ethel had recommended this place, assuring him that he would enjoy the experience. And it had, Ryan reflected, turned out to be just that—an experience. He had no idea if he'd ever visited an old-fashioned barbershop before, one that came complete with a candy-striped pole standing at the entrance, but they didn't exactly seem to be a common sight these days. Nonetheless, he couldn't deny that this one fit right in on Harmony's bustling Main Street, with a diner probably dating back to the fifties just down the block and a sturdy granite bank building that might qualify as a genuine landmark only yards away.

"Oh, I'm no youngster," Floyd allowed, "but my fingers are as nimble as ever."

"Doesn't seem as though anything's wrong with your feet, either," Ryan added as scissors clipped above him and dark strands fell to his cape-covered shoulders. "I saw you putting some rock-and-roll tunes to good use at Ethel's party."

A wide smile split Floyd's long face, showing a

row of teeth as white as his barber's coat. "Got to keep moving, especially when you're flirting with sixty. Otherwise, bones can get too set in their ways. Of course, you don't have to worry about that happening for a while."

Ryan pursed his lips. "I'm not so sure on that score. Someone recently told me that I wasn't as young as I used to be." *Not that I didn't do my damnedest last night to prove her wrong.*

Floyd paused and studied his customer in the mirror with a shrewdly assessing gaze his brown-rimmed glasses did nothing to hide. "You've got a long way to go, son. Barbers and bartenders being allowed to dispense advice, I'll offer some for what it's worth. Don't worry too much about time passing. That's almost guaranteed to age a person. It's always been a mystery to me why some folks seem obliged to push the clock forward." He shook a sandy-haired head generously threaded with gray. "For example, you take that retired army man staying at Aunt Abigail's."

Ryan's ears perked up. He suddenly felt more alert than he had all morning. "Major Hobbs?"

"Yep. He came in here to get a trim once. Had a nice head of hair. Thick and healthy."

"Uh-huh." Ryan ran his tongue around his teeth. "Ethel said she thought those silver streaks at his temples made him look distinguished."

"Guess that's true." Floyd shrugged a bony shoulder and went back to his task. "Maybe that's why he did it."

Ryan frowned. "Did what?"

"Dyed his hair. Probably a little while before he came in, too, because I could just make out the black roots. The funny thing is, if people choose to go that route, the tendency is to cover up any gray to make themselves look younger. They don't usually try to make themselves look older.''

Except the bogus major had apparently done just that, Ryan thought. Well, now he knew something else about the guy, even though it didn't seem all that helpful. Still, it occurred to him that it wouldn't hurt to ask some questions. Or one question, anyway. ''Did he, ah, happen to mention anything about the end of May?''

Floyd mulled that over for a second. ''Not to my recollection,'' he replied. ''Mostly we talked about travel spots in Arizona. He said it was his first visit to the state.''

''He told me that, too,'' Ryan murmured.

''The desert areas are a special favorite of mine,'' Floyd continued, ''so I recommended he check some of them out. He didn't intend to take my advice, though. Said any desert was sure to be too barren for him.'' The barber set the scissors down and ran a comb through Ryan's hair. ''The reason that particular piece of the conversation stuck in my mind, I imagine, was that when I went on to mention how not only one cactus tall enough to dwarf a man but miles of them stretched out to the horizon could be quite a sight, he called them saguaro.''

''Which,'' Ryan pointed out, ''they are.''

''True enough,'' Floyd agreed, ''but most folks from other parts of the country don't pronounce the name exactly right, not their first time here. That's why it struck me when he had it down pat. I even complimented him on it.''

''And what did he say?'' Ryan asked, keeping his voice level.

"Nothing that I can recall. Fact is, I don't remember him talking much at all after that."

Because he'd slipped? Ryan wondered. Because he was better acquainted with the desert than he'd meant to let on?

Who the hell knew?

Floyd removed the cape with a flourish. "You're done," he declared, stepping back.

Ryan sat forward and inspected the barber's work. "Nice job," he said, rising and turning from the mirror.

"Glad you like it." The older man's gaze again met Ryan's. All at once his eyes took on a twinkle that actually made him look far younger than his years. "You know, the real test of a haircut is to have a pretty woman run her fingers through it."

A smile tugged at Ryan's mouth. "No kidding? And then what happens?"

"Whatever you can sweet-talk her into, son."

Ryan was still smiling when he left the shop. He vowed to pay another visit to Abby's room that night and do his best to talk her into a whole bunch of things. Yes, indeed.

Then maybe they'd get some sleep…eventually.

ABBY FULLY EXPECTED her godmother to stop by Aunt Abigail's sometime on Saturday, even with the ongoing repair and remodeling efforts in progress at the Stockton ranch. Something told her that the sharp-eyed, sharp-witted woman wouldn't be able to stay away. Not today.

And she'd been right, Abby thought to herself when Gail walked into the narrow office wedged behind the center staircase, a windowless room that could be considered the business core of the bed-and-breakfast operation.

Here, as in the family area on the second floor, furnishings from a past era gave way to a small teak desk holding various computer equipment and topped by a clear fluorescent light, all of which were as contemporary, if on a somewhat less elaborate scale, as the contents of Abby's former office in a posh Phoenix resort. Here, she had immediately felt at home on her first day as stand-in manager at Aunt Abigail's, as though she and her talents fit right in and could be used to advantage.

And here, she supposed, was as good a place as any to deal with the information she more than suspected Ethel had already passed along via a hastily placed phone call—a suspicion readily confirmed by Gail's opening statement as she perched herself on one corner of the desk.

"So what's this I hear about the engagement being off?"

Abby lounged back in her leather swivel chair. As always, she had to admire her godmother's candid manner. For all that Gail and Abby's mother, Lillian, were longtime friends, their basic approach to conducting a conversation was by no means similar. Lillian had scant trouble weaving her way through most any discussion with diplomatic ease, probably a plus in a corporate wife and sophisticated hostess.

But despite Abby's considerable experience in the corporate world during her own career, she could appreciate Gail's blunt directness. With this woman, she thought, people never had much doubt about where they—and Gail—stood.

"If you heard that Allan and I agreed to disagree,

that's totally correct,'' Abby said mildly, repeating her earlier explanation.

''Hmm.'' Gail's gaze lit with a probing gleam as bright as the metal buttons on the chambray work shirt she wore with paint-stained chinos. ''And condolences don't seem to be in order.''

''No, they're not.'' Abby crossed one leg over the other. ''It was, as I'm sure Ethel wasted little time in mentioning, a mutual decision.''

Gail studied her goddaughter for a long moment, then issued a short sigh that spelled relief. ''She did say that, but I had to see for myself that you were okay. I haven't made much of a secret of the fact that I didn't think Allan was right for you, but I never wanted you to be hurt.''

Abby, well-acquainted with Gail's softer side, didn't question for an instant how true that was. ''I know,'' she said. ''I'm grateful for your concern, trust me, but there's no need. I really am fine.''

''Good.'' Gail smiled. ''And since that's been settled, I have to confess to hoping this will lead to your changing your mind about leaving Harmony.''

As it turned out, Abby had already given the matter some thought. It was the very reason she'd retreated to the office during Cara's afternoon nap. Calling on her more practical side, she'd made a mental list of the pros and cons. And in the end, the choice had been plain. Not only had she become genuinely fond of this city and many of its residents, she firmly believed she would be doing the right thing for Cara by remaining here.

''Well, you don't have to hope anymore,'' she said. ''I'm staying.''

Gail's smile widened. ''Then can I assume that I

have a new business partner and permanent manager for Aunt Abigail's?''

''You can,'' Abby replied without hesitation.

''Thank heavens.'' The older woman hopped from the desk and leaned over to give Abby a hug. ''Now that I'm certain you truly want to do this, I'll admit it's a big load off my mind, and I'll help make the move easier for you in any way I can.''

''Does that mean,'' Abby asked, raising a wry eyebrow as Gail straightened to gaze down at her, ''that you'll call my folks and break the news that their only daughter is not marrying the doctor of their dreams?''

A comical grimace crossed Gail's face. ''I don't want to help you that much.''

''Figures,'' Abby griped good-naturedly. ''After the initial shock waves rip through Tucson and ruffle the crystal-blue waters of their sculpted swimming pool, I'll have to listen to them trying not to sound too gloomy when we both know they're going to be badly disappointed.''

Gail's expression sobered. ''I'm presuming they have no idea that your ex-husband is here.''

''None.'' Abby decided to be a bit blunt herself, fully aware that Gail knew Abby's parents had never been thrilled with the man their daughter *had* married. ''And I'd rather they didn't find out,'' she said. ''I haven't brought up the subject during the few conversations I've had with them lately, and since they would never think to ask me directly about his whereabouts, my conscience isn't bothering me for leaving them in the dark.''

Gail nodded. ''When your mother calls me, which she's bound to do after you pass along your news, I'll respect your wishes, of course. And as for myself, I certainly don't plan on butting into your personal affairs.''

Abby gave her a meaningful look. "Really?"

In typical fashion, Gail was swift on the uptake. "All right, so Ethel and I did meddle a little when Ryan first arrived."

Abby wasn't about to let her off the hook. "Do you actually consider trying to throw the two of us together at every opportunity to be meddling a *little?*"

Gail rolled her eyes. "Okay, maybe more than a little, which I hereby promise to stop doing as of this minute." She hesitated, as though debating whether to go on before she spoke again. "But, meddling aside, I'd be less than honest if I didn't say that I can't help wondering how much you still care for Ryan."

Abby knew no response was required. If she chose to drop the matter, her godmother wouldn't press her. Nevertheless, something compelled her to say, "I do have feelings for him." She paused. "Maybe more than it's wise for me to have."

Once again Gail's small features settled into serious lines. "How do you think he feels?" she asked.

Abby lifted one shoulder in a slight shrug. "I'm not sure."

Which was true enough, she told herself. At the moment all she was completely certain of where Ryan's feelings were concerned was that he had no qualms about making love with her.

"But no matter how he feels," she went on in the next breath, "everything could change in a heartbeat."

Gail's expression turned thoughtful. "You mean when—or if—his memory returns?"

"I don't think there's any *if* about it," Abby said as a vivid image of the flash of the old Ryan she'd seen the night before formed in her mind. Although it soon faded, she remained convinced of the ultimate outcome. "His memory will come back. It's just a question of when."

"And until then...?" Gail's voice trailed off.

Abby did her best to maintain an even tone. "Until then he'll probably stay in Harmony," she finished. "I can't deny that he seems to like it here." *But that might well be because he isn't the same person he was,* she could have added. *Once his memory returns, once he has the whole of himself back, then things may be far different.*

At that point, as she'd told her godmother, everything could change in a heartbeat.

So, when it came to the most private part of her life, she would concentrate on the here and now. That, Abby had to conclude, was the best way to handle the situation. As long as she could take it one day at a time, as long as she didn't get in too deep, as long as she didn't let herself care *too* much, she could enjoy what she had.

In the here and now, as startling as it still might seem, she and Ryan were again intimately involved. *But not firmly committed.* Not this time.

Regardless of what happened in the coming days, the commitment they'd once made to each other no longer applied. It was over. As over as their marriage.

Chapter Ten

"I've been thinking about this divorce," Ryan said several nights later, as he lounged flat on his stomach in bed with only a sheet covering him. "I mean, you and me and how we wound up on opposite sides in court," he added, and didn't miss the way the woman stretched out on her back beside him seemed to stiffen slightly at his words.

"The divorce," she told him after a silent moment, "is long over."

Ryan propped his head on an elbow and studied Abby in the light of the bedside lamp as she stared up at the ceiling, her tousled red hair a sharp contrast to the snowy-white pillow. "Yeah," he agreed, "but I still have to wonder about it."

Which was no lie, he thought. During the past few days he'd found his curiosity concerning that particular time in both their lives steadily growing. What had really happened? he'd asked himself more than once.

It wasn't a question of their being physically incompatible; that much he knew full well. Just minutes earlier they'd made love again. And again it had been terrific—for both of them, a firm conclusion his ego had little to do with forming. The way Abby had shivered in his arms, moaned against his mouth and finally shuddered along the whole length of him in release had confirmed her pleasure without words and provided another demonstration of the fact that physically they were compatible right down to the ground.

No, whatever their past problems had been, sex had not been one of them. Still, as thoroughly satisfying as the prospect might be, two people couldn't make love all the time, Ryan conceded. They had to sleep sometimes and eat on a regular basis in order to survive, plus, unless they were independently wealthy, they had to work to put food on the table.

And how he'd felt about his choice of work had apparently been a problem. A big one.

"From what I gather," he said, "flying was important to me, important enough that my preoccupation with it drove a wedge between us." He kept his gaze on Abby. "Is that a fair summary of the situation?"

Abby released a quiet sigh, looking far from pleased with the current conversational turn. Her own gaze remained fixed on the creamy ceiling overhead as she dipped her chin in the briefest of nods.

"And that's what led to the breakup?"

"Basically," she replied after a short moment.

Basically. It was exactly what she'd told him on another occasion, Ryan recalled. On the back porch, just before he'd kissed her for the first time in years, and just after he'd pushed for an answer to his then-newly-formed theory that long days spent in the air and away from her had prompted their divorce, she'd said "basically."

Then and now, it might simply have been a way to

put a quick halt to the discussion. Or maybe—just maybe, he mused—there'd been more to the breakup than his urge to fly.

"And what does 'basically' mean?" he asked.

That had Abby slanting a glance at him. Rather than displaying any sign of yielding to his question, however, her smoky-green gaze held a stubborn glint. "Ryan, I'm not getting into this," she said, her tone matching her expression. "As far as I'm concerned, there's absolutely no point in it, so please do us both a favor and let it go."

He didn't want to let it go. But it was her choice, he reminded himself, and a smart man would probably take that reminder to heart. *Start pushing too much and she may just push you straight out of her bed, Larabee.*

Deciding that was the last thing he wanted, Ryan blew out a breath. "Okay, I'll just shut up," he muttered.

Somewhat to his amazement, that won him a small smile as Abby tucked an edge of the sheet under her arm and turned his way. "Thank you."

He arched a brow. "For shutting up?"

Her smile grew. "No, for respecting my wishes."

He had to smile himself as he let his head drop back on the pillow to rest in the circle of his arms. "Just like a sensitive man would do, huh?"

"Yes." She reached out a hand and brushed a silky-skinned palm down his spine, taking the sheet covering his back with it. "And it occurs to me that a sensitive man might appreciate a soothing back-rub."

Thanks to Lively, his back*side* was what needed soothing, but Ryan had no intention of pointing that out. In his opinion, even sensitive men didn't whine about every little ache and pain. And to a woman? No way.

Nevertheless, despite his resolve to say nothing, it didn't take Abby long to remark on that particular portion of his anatomy when she leaned forward and lowered the sheet several more inches. "You've got bruises in some very interesting places," she told him, then added after a beat, "I have to admit I've been wondering about what might have been causing them for days now."

"Hmm." It seemed the shoe was on the other foot, Ryan thought, and now she was curious about something only he could answer. Well, that wasn't entirely true, he acknowledged. The owners of a certain ranch could have brought her up to speed in record time, and even Lively could have spilled the beans if the bull had developed a talent for telling tales in addition to a knack for lifting a haughty nose at a rider's failure to meet exacting standards.

Whatever the case, though, Ryan decided he was keeping mum. Maybe if he'd been successful in making it to the full eight seconds, he'd have chosen otherwise and bragged a little. But he hadn't, dammit. He was close, so close, achieving seven seconds more often than not before Lively bucked him off and had him biting the dust. Too bad seven wasn't the magic number on the rodeo circuit.

"It seems like you have your secrets, so I'll keep mine," he said mildly, slanting a one-eyed glance up at Abby while his other eye rested shut against the pillow. "But feel free to rub wherever you want. Ah, anywhere at all."

She laughed softly, clearly getting his drift. "Anywhere as in everywhere?"

"Uh-huh."

"Are you prepared for what's bound to happen if I take you up on that?"

He chuckled, a rumble of sound. "Why don't you start rubbing and we'll see?"

As IT WORKED OUT, Ryan was able, not to mention ready and willing, to tackle another round of bedroom activities. Then it was his turn to stare at the ceiling, this time in the darkness, when Abby finally gave in to sleep. He knew he should be getting some rest himself, and probably would be if thoughts of their earlier conversation hadn't started to nag at him again.

What possible reason other than his preoccupation with flying could have helped land the Larabees in divorce court? Provided there actually had been another reason, of course. Cripes, he couldn't even be sure of that much, not with his memory currently telling him squat.

Nonetheless, sheer common sense said that he and Abby must have had something major going for them, at least in the beginning. After all, they'd entered into a marriage that was far from one of convenience, so they must have cared about each other. More than a little, too.

And she still cared.

He could be dead certain on that point, since she'd told him so straight out the night her engagement had come to a rapid end—an engagement she'd been ready to end herself because she continued to have feelings for him. As to exactly how he'd once felt, he had no clue. But right this minute? Yes, he cared about her, Ryan couldn't deny. It wasn't just that he wanted Abby. *He cared.*

The question was: Where did they go from here?

It was a hard one to answer. Especially on his part, Ryan allowed with a frown, given that where he'd come from was still more or less a mystery to him. The truth was that no matter how many things people told him about himself, a gut-deep feeling remained that part of him was lost. He could only hope he'd be able to find it soon.

Just then Ryan heard a small noise coming from the connecting room. Had to be the baby, he thought. He hadn't heard a sound from that direction during all the earlier nights he'd spent here. Even when he'd dragged himself out of bed before the birds were up to head back to his own room, it had been quiet.

Why he'd felt obliged to repeatedly drag himself out of bed before dawn was a puzzle he hadn't quite figured out himself, other than that for some reason the early morning seemed like a personal time between mother and child. A time when he could be considered an outsider? Maybe.

Regardless, though, the fact remained that the baby had always spent a peaceful night. Until now.

And did that mean there was a problem?

Deciding he wouldn't wake Abby up unless something really was wrong, Ryan eased himself away from her and rose to his feet. He snagged his jeans from a nearby chair and pulled them on. Moonlight slipping through the sheer bedroom curtains lit his path as he moved as silently as possible across the room. He gave the door a slight push, then poked his head in and had no trouble making out a white crib and its occupant in the muted glow of a small night-light.

Cara lay with her eyes shut tight, her brow knitted and her hands moving restlessly across the top of a yellow blanket. The way she was whimpering was what had drawn his notice, Ryan knew.

"Must be a bad dream," he mumbled under his breath as he stepped into the room. He could readily sympathize. He'd had more than a few full-blown nightmares himself after his accident. Though whatever was bothering the baby didn't seem to be anywhere near that serious. "Might have had too much to eat," he told himself. One corner of his mouth slanted up. The kid could sure chow down.

He walked forward with hushed steps, but as quiet as his movements were, the baby's dark eyes popped open as he came to a halt beside the crib. "It's only me," he told her softly. Leaning in, he reached down a hand and patted one of hers in reassurance. "There's nothing to worry about. You can go back to sleep."

All at once she smiled up at him, just the briefest, softest smile. Surprisingly, it was enough to have something stirring in his chest. Before he could even begin to wonder about the unfamiliar sensation, she closed her eyes and issued a tiny sigh. It didn't take him long to recognize that she'd heeded his advice and was headed back to sleep.

"That's it," Ryan said in encouragement, lowering his voice another notch. "You don't have to be afraid. You have plenty of people to look out for you. In fact, you are one lucky little girl, because you get to grow up in the gingerbread house."

Which was another thing he could be sure of, Ryan

thought. Whatever details Abby might or might not be keeping under wraps about the past, she'd made no secret of her recent decision to stay in Harmony and manage the bed and breakfast. Ethel had been as pleased as punch at the news. So had Gail when he'd seen her at the ranch. Even Bill had pronounced it to be a "damn fine idea."

And it probably was, Ryan admitted, leaving the smaller bedroom as quietly as he'd come in. Abby had a clear-cut plan for the future, and it appeared to be a good one. As to how her former husband might fit in, Ryan could only figure that remained to be seen. Not that he had any desire to let things between them just drift along. Once he had the lost part of himself back, he wanted to make some decisions of his own.

Right now, though, he'd flat-out better get some rest. And with that reflection Ryan undressed and slid back into bed. He'd barely closed his eyes when Abby spoke, her voice no more than a murmur. "Is everything all right?"

"Yes." He reached out and pulled her to him, suddenly feeling very protective. Very, he supposed with some self-directed amusement, macho male. "Everything's fine," he said. "Go back to sleep."

For the second time in minutes, a female didn't hesitate to take him at his word.

"YES, WE'LL have to stock up on flour and other baking supplies in a major way, because business is definitely picking up." Sure of her words, Abby tapped her pen on the thick pad of paper she held, and reclined in one of the back-porch wicker chairs. Ryan sat in a second chair, booted feet stretched out in front of him, while Ethel was settled on the sunflower-print sofa with Cara, who was caught up in the wonders of a colorful fabric children's book.

Abby had been conducting a short planning session with Aunt Abigail's cook when Ryan joined them on his return from spending another morning at the Stockton ranch. Abby knew he'd been helping Bill around the place, since no one had made any mystery of that fact. What she didn't know was why she suspected something else might be involved in those visits. But regardless of her suspicions, she had no intention of asking Ryan about it, especially after their conversation the night before and what seemed to be a joint agreement on their right to keep things to themselves.

What she did intend to do, and right this minute, was get a good start on her new job responsibilities before the busiest time of the year hit. "If reservations keep coming in as they have lately," she said, "we're going to be booked all summer."

"As we usually are," Ethel remarked with satisfaction.

"Which is why I want to be sure we're prepared." Abby went back to her list. "I've checked on supplies needed upstairs, and it looks as though we're all set when it comes to bedroom and bathroom basics, such as linens, towels, bath mats and extra liners for the lace shower curtains."

"Don't forget the fancy lavender soap," Ryan slid in dryly.

It earned him an amused look from Ethel. "We'll make certain there's plenty. We know that's your special favorite, and we wouldn't want you to do without."

"Ouch." His features twisted in a mock wince. "I

suppose I'll take that as a hint to just keep quiet until you women finish your plans."

A smile tugged at Abby's lips before she returned to the matter at hand and studied the thorough inventory she'd taken. "What we will need soon are some additional room fresheners and another case of disposable drinking cups."

Ethel nodded. "I'll put those on the shopping list. Anything else?"

"Not that I can come up with at the moment. And since we've already dealt with the downstairs areas, I think that's it." Abby dropped the pad of paper into her lap. "Starting Friday, we'll have a full house with all the visitors coming for the rodeo, and if history repeats itself, things probably won't slow down much from then until fall."

"I'm so glad you'll be here," Ethel said, her voice cheerfully displaying the truth of that. "You seem to have a gift for organization."

She did, and Abby saw no reason to deny it. She took pride in her abilities and had learned to put them to good use, something her parents had always encouraged in their children. In addition to her personal accomplishments in the working world, both her brothers had become successful businessmen, so the value of that parental guidance certainly could not be argued.

Her older siblings had also made good marriages that had led to their own growing families. And there, she'd fallen short of her parents' expectations, Abby knew. Oh, they'd handled the announcement of her ex-engagement fairly well. Still, unmistakable disappointment had underscored their words as much as they'd tried for an upbeat tone.

If she had offered details about how Allan had found himself flung head over heels—and purple heels, to boot—into a torrid affair with his nurse, they would probably have been shocked to their toes. And if she had mentioned who'd been seated beside her when Allan broke the news, they just might have swallowed their tongues.

Luckily, Abby reflected, she hadn't gone into details.

"—so I think you and Ryan should go to the rodeo dance Friday night," Ethel was saying when Abby tuned back into the discussion.

She straightened in her chair. The idea of a small night on the town held appeal, Abby had to admit. But other things had to come first. "It's going to be busy here Friday," she pointed out, "plus there's Cara to consider."

Ethel waved a casual hand in dismissal. "Everyone will have checked in before it's time for you to leave, and I can watch the little darling. It will be no trouble at all." She reached over to gently tickle one of the baby's tiny knees and received a small giggle in response.

"You're not going to the shindig?" Ryan asked. "I thought you were the big dancer in this group."

Laughing lightly, Ethel aimed a glance his way. "I did enough of that on my birthday to last me for quite a while." She returned her gaze to Abby. "Cara can spend the night with me in my room. We'll put her playpen in there, add some blankets for padding, and she'll sleep like a top. You won't even have to worry about getting up too early the next day. I can fix her cereal for her."

Abby frowned slightly, debating how to reply. On

one hand, she had no doubt about the fact that Cara would be perfectly fine with Ethel and might even enjoy a minor change in routine. On the other, she had no desire to impose on the older woman. "Are you certain you want to do this?"

A bright smile lit Ethel's face. "Land sakes, yes."

Reassured, Abby looked at Ryan. "Are you game?"

He shrugged a shoulder. "I guess. Then again, I'm not even sure I can dance."

Brief scenes of the past flitted through her mind, one after the other. Scenes of her held in a pair of strong arms. Scenes of him grinning down at his partner as he moved with ease and grace, always in step with the beat.

"Trust me," she said with confidence, "you can dance."

HE COULD DANCE. Abby had been right on that score, Ryan decided. One turn around a crowded floor holding her close while he led them through a small sea of gliding bodies had gone a long way toward making that clear.

"Told you so," she said, gazing up at him with a knowing look, as though she'd read his thoughts. "You may have been born tapping your toes."

"Could be," he allowed mildly, although the truth was that he couldn't even imagine himself as a child, much less a newborn. "But this is a slow song. When the band perks things up, I suppose that'll be the real test."

"You'll pass."

He smoothly avoided another collision. "Even if I'm not as young as I used to be?"

She rolled her eyes. "I'm beginning to believe I created a monster by telling you that. Just don't try to keep this up until we both drop to prove me wrong."

"Okay, I'll give you a break," he agreed after pretending to consider the matter. "Still, it wouldn't do this shindig justice if we didn't celebrate along with the rest of this happy group. Or maybe I should say rowdy bunch."

"The Wild West," Abby reminded him, "was a rowdy place."

And tonight some of Harmony's citizens had done their best to bring a part of it to life, Ryan thought. The large gym at the local community center had been transformed into a frontier dancehall complete with lettered signs of the era decorating the walls, including one warning that the sheriff took exception to indoor gunplay, and a sturdy oak bar that was so long, it must have been brought into the building in pieces and reassembled.

Bartenders sporting thick fake mustaches, and cocktail waitresses colorfully decked out in barmaid costumes of vivid satin bolstered the image, while people throughout the room wearing fashions in tune with the theme looked thoroughly comfortable in the setting. All but one person. His partner, Ryan couldn't help but note, hardly seemed at ease with her current mode of dress.

"You are one cute cowgirl," he didn't hesitate to tell her.

That earned him another roll of Abby's eyes. "Why in the world did I let my godmother talk me into wearing this?"

He ran his tongue around his teeth. "Weak moment?"

"Weak thinking, maybe," she admitted.

"Well, I like the outfit."

"Humph. Easy for you to be so cheerful about the whole thing. You got away with opening a closet door and pulling out the same white shirt and black pants you wore at Ethel's party."

"They're cut along Western lines," he pointed out. "You, on the other hand, apparently didn't have much resembling that style in your closet."

She released a thin sigh. "Nothing anywhere near similar, unfortunately."

So Gail Stockton had come up with a ruby-red shirt with diamond-studded snaps and a pair of fancy, far-from-conservative blue jeans, both of which she'd borrowed from the daughter of a friend. Luckily, Ryan thought with amusement, he'd been around to see Abby's face when she'd first laid eyes on them. *Appalled* might be too strong a description. But it was close.

"I know it's not the kind of stuff you're used to wearing," he said, gliding them past a band that was clearly geared up for the occasion. Most of its members looked as much like gunfighters as musicians.

Abby followed him in a turn, moving as effortlessly as he did. "At least I didn't let Gail convince me to buy boots. My navy flats are fine. I probably should have bought my own jeans, though," she grumbled, "because these are too tight."

"Trust me," he said, echoing her confident tone when she'd assured him of his dancer potential, "they're not too tight."

In his opinion, they weren't only just right but also

a damn good sight, molding themselves to her lower body and long legs like a glove. Some ruby-red high heels would have probably capped the picture off nicely, but he was pretty sure she didn't have any of those in her closet, either.

"I don't doubt that the way they fit leaves little to the imagination," Abby murmured.

"Uh-huh. And my only complaint is that those denim-clad hips and the shiny stars stitched on some well-placed back pockets are winning you more than a bit of attention from the younger male crowd."

"Really?" Abby lifted a brow, recalling a time when she'd opted for jeans on a regular basis, before giving them up in favor of less casual clothing that seemed to go along with her increasing responsibilities in the business world. She'd worn red as well, sizzling red, not caring a whit that it clashed with her hair.

But that was then; this was now. And, unless she was mistaken, Ryan had been enjoying her discomfort a little too much.

Deciding she'd read the signals correctly, Abby set about providing a dash of distress to the guilty party. "The younger men. My goodness. Do you suppose they'll ask me to dance?" she asked oh-so-innocently as the song wound to an end.

He frowned at that, but before he could reply, the Stocktons approached them. Like Ryan, Bill needed no more than his usual Western garb to fit right in, but Gail had chosen to go with a period dress made of toffee-colored silk that featured a high-necked, fitted bodice and wide, flowing skirt.

Gail offered them a smile. "Are you two having a good time?"

"I was up until a second ago," Ryan muttered under his breath.

Swallowing a chuckle because she'd been just close enough to catch that, Abby said, "Yes, indeed."

"Me, too," Bill chimed in.

"And by that he means he's had a chance to ogle all the barmaids," his wife explained dryly.

"Now, honeybun—"

"You know it's true," she told him, breaking in. "But I'm in such a great mood that I suppose I'll have to forgive you."

Bill launched an assessing look, as though judging if she really meant it, then gave her a long, slow wink. "You are one downright fine woman."

Gail laughed. "Why don't you dance with Abby," she suggested, "and I'll let Ryan twirl me around the room."

Everyone agreed with that plan, and Abby soon found herself following Bill across the floor. He wasn't as good a dancer as her last partner, but then, she suspected, not many men were. Nevertheless, the older man could hold his own, as he proved with quick steps that kept in time with an upbeat country tune.

"There seems to be a good turnout this evening," Abby said after a minute. "With all the work she put into planning this, Gail must be pleased."

Bill dipped his head in a brief nod. "Enough, I guess, that she didn't make much fuss about my, uh, admiring some of the costumes."

This time Abby gave in to a quiet chuckle as she aimed a sweeping glance over the room. "Even if we discount the barmaids who you were 'admiring,' there are a lot of younger women here.'' And younger men, she reminded herself with amusement.

''Plenty of the newer generation out tonight,'' Bill agreed. ''Being away from here as long I have, I don't know all that many of them, but we can get Gail to introduce you around.''

''I think,'' Abby said slowly after a moment's pause, ''I'd enjoy that very much.''

But whether her date would enjoy the possible results remained to be seen.

''WHO THE DEVIL is she dancing with now?'' Ryan propped an elbow on the bar and tried not to scowl. It wasn't easy.

Bill took a swallow from his frosted mug of cold beer and craned his neck for a better look at the couples on the floor. ''Well, that's someone I do happen to recognize. He's Tom Kennedy's nephew, his sister's boy.''

''Hardly a boy,'' Ryan groused, studying the male in question.

''Probably not more than twenty-five,'' Bill pointed out.

And, Ryan added silently, the latest in a string of twentysomethings who had invited *his* date to take a spin around the room. Sure, he'd managed more than a few dances with her himself. But not nearly enough to suit him.

''I figured Tom might be here tonight,'' Bill said, ''but I suppose with the parade tomorrow and then the rodeo, plus all the visitors and extra traffic to deal with, the local police chief has his work cut out for him.''

Ryan blew out a breath and pulled his gaze from

Abby and her partner. "I know I still have my work cut out for me if I'm going to get the best of that bull of yours." Something he hadn't yet done, at least not according to Bill's stopwatch and Lively's inner timer. And the big day wasn't far off. The bull-riding competition would be the last of the events to be held on Sunday afternoon.

Bill gave him a shrewd look, as though recognizing his continued frustration in that area. "Have you let Abby in on your project yet?"

"No."

"Going to invite her to come with you on Sunday?"

Perhaps to see him come up short one more time? Ryan reflected ruefully. "I'm still debating it." Which was the sheer truth, and he wasn't all that certain of the outcome.

"Ask her."

The brisk, no-nonsense tone of that short statement had Ryan raising a brow. "Why would it make a difference if she's there or not?"

Bill's gaze didn't waver. "Because a man can always use a little incentive, no matter how good he is at what he does. And I've got more than a hunch that knowing she's in the stands watching will give you the edge you need."

"Hmm." Ryan took a long sip of his beer. "I'll think about it," he said at last.

"You do that," Bill told him, smiling his wily smile. "Just keep in mind that I didn't get to be as old as I am without learning a few things." He paused. "Now, they're about to wind this song down, and if you don't want her snatched away from you again, you'd better get moving."

Ryan set his mug on the bar with a quiet *clunk*. "There," he said with firm intent, "I'm taking your advice."

Turning on one boot heel, he left the older man and started across the room. By the time the current tune ended, he was halfway past the stage the band occupied. "Got a request, cowboy?" someone called out.

Ryan stopped in his tracks and glanced up at the lead singer, who fixed him with a stare worthy of a showdown at high noon. Then the man ruined it with a companionable curve of thin lips surrounded by scruffy dark beard.

"Can we play something for you and your special gal?" the man drawled.

Ryan didn't have to think twice. It just popped into his head. "How about 'Lady in Red'?"

The singer mulled that over. "Not exactly a country favorite," he pointed out, "but I think we can oblige you." After a hasty discussion with his band mates, he turned back to Ryan. "Okay, find your gal and we'll tune up."

He found her. Just in the nick of time, too, Ryan noted, watching another of the younger males make a beeline over to where Abby stood talking to another woman.

"Sorry," Ryan said mildly, cutting the guy off without a qualm. "The next dance is mine."

And with that he took Abby's elbow and led her back to the floor without so much as a backward look at the man he'd thwarted. Let him get his own woman, Ryan thought with satisfaction.

"I guess I don't get a say-so in this whole thing," Abby remarked, humor underscoring her words.

"Not this time," he told her, keeping his tone mild.

"The band asked me to pick out a special tune for us."

The music began then, and for the first time that evening Abby missed a beat as Ryan started them off. He glanced down at her. "Getting tired?"

"No," she replied after the barest pause. "I'm fine." Regaining her usual grace, she followed as he held her close. They were only steps into the dance when she spoke again. "You asked the band to play this song?"

"Uh-huh."

She considered that for a second. "Any particular reason?"

"Not really. It just seemed appropriate."

Abby rested her chin on his shoulder. "It probably seemed that way because of what I'm wearing," she murmured, so quietly that she might have been talking to herself.

And she could well be right, he had to admit as the music swelled to fill the room. After all, what other reason could there be? Why else would he have picked a song that was hardly a match for the current setting?

Then all at once he knew exactly why he'd made that choice as a vivid scene formed in his mind.

Him and Abby dancing.

But in a place far different.

And at a time far distant.

Yet to this very same song.

Back then, as now, she was dressed in something that brightened the deep scarlet highlights in her hair and turned it to every shade of the sunset. Back then, as now, she was a woman vibrantly framed in red.

Back then, as now, she was his very own—

Ryan broke off that thought and brought them to a smooth halt in the middle of the crowded floor. Still holding Abby close in the circle of one arm, he tipped her chin up with his other hand and locked his gaze to hers.

"You're every bit as lovely," he told her softly, "as you were on the night I met you...crimson lady."

Chapter Eleven

Crimson lady. His name for her from their very first dance. No one else had ever called her that. Just him.

For a moment, Abby could only stare. Then she managed to swallow and finally to speak. "You remembered."

He nodded. "Something, at any rate. A good look at the evening we met just surfaced out of nowhere." Somehow, although Abby was barely aware of it, he got them moving again to the music's steady beat. "The doctors said it would probably play out like this, that my memory wouldn't return all at once, but in pieces."

And what would happen when he had all of it back? Abby wondered. What then?

No, she told herself in the next breath, this wasn't the time for speculation. This was a moment to simply be happy for him, and she was.

"Nevertheless, it's a start," she said, summoning a smile, "and that's wonderful."

He offered a small smile of his own. "I do recall that after I got you in my arms that night, I made sure no one else had a chance to break things up." His jaw tightened as a determined expression settled on his face. "So consider this fair warning. The next guy who tries to waltz you away from me will find himself meeting some stiff resistance."

Realizing he meant it, Abby judged it in everyone's best interests to give in on that point. Still, she hesitated, as though weighing the matter, before saying, "I believe I've done all the dancing I want to do with anyone else."

"Good thing," Ryan said in a near-growl that had her fighting to hide her secret pleasure at his reaction.

"You always were a tad possessive," she told him. *But I never so much as looked at another man after I met you.* She could have voiced that thought, and didn't, recognizing how much it would stroke his male ego.

"And how about you? Were you a bit possessive, too?"

"Oh, I'll confess to the occasional urge to indulge in a hair-pulling contest when some woman was blatantly licking her chops over you," she said lightly, and knew she'd stroked his ego after all by the sudden gratified glint in his gaze.

He leaned in and brought his lips to her ear. "Your hair was longer on the night we met."

"So was yours," she informed him. "I could run my fingers through it where it brushed against your collar." Abby rubbed a hand over the warm skin at that same spot. "It's probably cooler this way, though."

"I suppose so. Maybe that's why I had it cut shorter. It was already starting to heat up down south when I left there." He pressed a soft, open-mouthed kiss to her temple. "And as I remember, it was downright hot outside on the night I first laid eyes on you."

"Very," she acknowledged even as her temperature rose a notch. "It was far from cold on that dance floor, too."

"You suggested we sit for a while and talk—"

"—but you were content to keep dancing," she finished.

Ryan pulled back slightly and looked down at her. "Only because I didn't want to let go of you."

Abby met his gaze. "And what do you want now?"

"You." He released a gusty breath. "Cripes, who am I kidding? Holding you close like this, which is not nearly close enough, is flat-out driving me crazy. I highly recommend that we get the hell out of here."

She had to smile again. "How quickly do you think we can get back to Aunt Abigail's?"

"I plan on making it in record time," he said in a husky voice. "And then I plan on making love to you until you beg me to stop."

A sigh of anticipation broke from her throat. "It's a deal."

RYAN DIDN'T SPEED down the dark roads as fast as some parts of him urged, but they still arrived back at the bed and breakfast in short order. He was grateful to see that all looked quiet when Abby used her key to enter the house. With no guests around, he thought to himself, he wouldn't have to try to nudge anyone into heading off to bed tonight. All he had to do was get Abby to hers.

"I need to check in with Ethel," she told him, "just to make sure everything's all right. I'll be as quick as I can."

He nodded his agreement and started to pace the

hall as she left him to head toward the rear of the house. A fever of impatience he couldn't manage to damp down rose with each step. He'd begun to remember more of the past along the drive back, and it had all featured scenes of him and Abby stretched out on a king-size bed that took up a large portion of a small apartment bedroom. Night after night he'd reached for her, and she'd gone willingly, eagerly into his arms.

Ryan drew in a long breath and groped for his control. To give himself something to do, he switched off the hallway lights, leaving only one at the top of the center staircase lit. And then he could only continue his pacing.

After what seemed like forever but was probably no more than a couple of minutes, Abby returned. "I peeked into Ethel's room. Both she and Cara are sound asleep."

"And now you're all mine," he said, catching her close.

She wrapped her arms around his neck. "For the rest of the night."

Vowing to make the most of it, he picked her up and mounted the stairs. It didn't take him long to get them to her room and behind closed doors. Then he put her back on her feet beside the bed, switched on the lamp and set about removing every scrap of clothing they both wore. Starting with hers, he unsnapped her shirt and thanked his lucky stars that he didn't have to deal with a row of delicate buttons.

Abby wasted no time in returning the favor, springing his pearl snaps open with ease. "There's something to be said for the Western style," she said as she pushed his shirt back to reveal his chest.

"Damn right," he agreed, uncovering her lacy white bra.

Both shirts were soon discarded, along with Abby's bra. Shoes and boots followed, but when it came to a pair of fancy blue jeans, Ryan found himself faced with a formidable obstacle. "How did you get into these?" he asked, doing his best to peel the soft denim down her hips. And failing.

"It wasn't easy." Abby sucked in a breath. "I told you they were too tight."

"They're not too tight when they're on, just when it's time to get them off."

She shook her head over that piece of male logic. Ryan raked his fingers through his hair. "Okay, so I'm not making sense. Just try lying on the bed."

She did, and that worked, eventually, as his avid hands exposed the creamy skin of her lower body inch by inch. Ryan was sweating, for more reasons than one, by the time he was able to strip off his pants and dark briefs. He dived into bed in the next second, and lacy white panties were the last to go.

"Finally," he said. And then his mouth came down on hers.

There was nothing tentative about the kiss. Rather, from the moment their lips met, needs flared to life. Yes, there was a spark between them, Ryan thought. Just as there had been on the night they'd first met…and first touched.

Now, heat swiftly built, and flames rose to lick at the last traces of his restraint. He resisted, but not for long. The potent craving for release was simply too strong.

"I can't take it slow," he said as he broke the kiss

at last. His breath was ragged, a harsh sound in the quiet all around them.

"You don't have to take it slow." Abby gasped out the words, meaning every one. She had never been more ready in her life, she knew, to make love with this man.

"Next time will be different." Ryan reached into the nightstand drawer, retrieved protection and applied it. "Next time I'll draw it out and make good on my promise to have you begging."

But Abby wasn't thinking about the next time. Her skin felt as if it were on fire, and she wanted him— needed him—right this minute. When he came down on top of her, she put her arms around him and held on for all she was worth.

"Don't hold back," she said urgently. "Don't hold anything back."

He didn't. Instead he slipped inside, instantly found the ancient rhythm and never missed a beat.

"You're as good at this as you are at dancing," she managed to get out before the power of speech deserted her entirely. Then she could only feel, and what she felt was almost beyond description. Somewhere at the core of her, she knew Ryan felt it, too.

In this, they were one, she thought. In this, they were—always had been—in complete accord.

And so now, moving as one, hearts pounding and eyes locked on each other, they fanned the blaze roaring through them both, then purposely fed it until it rose to new heights.

Finally, they quenched it.

Sometime later Abby's sense of awareness returned. Her arms remained wrapped around the man stretched full-length on top of her; her lips were at his ear. "Next time I get to be on top," she murmured. "It's easier to breathe."

He groaned and shifted, allowing her lungs to fill as he levered himself downward and rested his head on her breasts.

She sighed a contented sigh. "We just may have broken some speed records, after all. And not the kind that have anything to do with cars."

"Yes, and all things considered I think it went fairly well," he said.

She dipped her chin and stared down at him. "Fairly well? We all but turn each other inside out, and you think it went *fairly well?*"

He raised his head, grinned. "Gotcha."

Again it was a flash of the old Ryan, who had always known how to play in bed. Abby supposed she'd better get used to it. With his memory returning, so, she imagined, would different facets of his personality. Thankfully, this was a side of him she had once found charming—and still did, she had to admit.

"When I get my turn on top," she warned archly, "I am definitely going to make you eat those words."

He narrowed his gaze in a wicked challenge. "And I'm still planning to make you beg before it's all over."

As it turned out, he nibbled on more than his words—a lot more—and she did wind up begging. Before they both drifted into sleep, an exhausted Abby said, "Thank heavens, we don't have to get up early."

"Amen to that," Ryan muttered in the darkness. "I'm ready to sleep like a log."

HE SLEPT. But not peacefully. Dreams mixed with memories chased him through what remained of the night. The ranch on a flat stretch of Wyoming where he'd grown up, the mother who had lovingly spoiled him, the sister who had been called upon to raise him after his mother's death, the father who had been forced to give up plans to pass along a legacy to his only son.

Something in the back of his mind told him that those same images, together with a vivid one of the woman he'd once called wife, had raced through his thoughts at the very moment his helicopter had plunged to sandy earth in the grip of a sudden wind-whipped storm. And, as other images emerged, it also told him what had brought him to that particular part of the desert.

He no longer had to wonder. He knew.

Ryan sat straight up in bed even as his eyes flashed open to meet the bare beginnings of another dawn. With the top sheet pooled at his waist, he rubbed a hand over his chest, more to assure himself that he was really awake than anything else.

His startled movement must have also woken Abby, because she was suddenly sitting beside him, clutching an edge of the sheet to her breasts and leaning forward to study him in the traces of light slipping in through the bedroom windows.

"What's wrong?" she asked after one look at his face.

Ryan let out a lengthy breath, then softly issued a sober statement. "I just remembered what's scheduled to happen the last weekend in May...*this* weekend."

She stared, eyes wide, at that news. "I take it,"

she said after a moment, "that it isn't anything good."

He frowned in thought. "Not necessarily," he told her. "It all depends on whether I can do something about it." He reached up and flicked back stray strands of hair hanging over his forehead. "I guess I should start at the beginning, which as it turns out goes back to the Sonora Lounge. Mac Dempsey was right on that score."

"That's the place where you two met the night before the accident?"

"Yes. He was ready to go in when I walked out, but the whole thing really started when I decided to stop by the bar for a beer after I'd finished having dinner there." Ryan pictured the scene in his mind. "Two guys were already sitting there when I sat down a couple of stools away. Business types, I thought, since they wore suits and ties. It was pretty plain that one of them had been drinking more than his share. He kept raising his voice—not to a shout, but just loud enough for me to catch a few slurred sentences now and then. The guy he was with kept glancing around the place and trying to shut him up, but I caught enough to whet my curiosity."

"And it was something to do with the end of May?" Abby ventured quietly.

Ryan nodded. "As far as I could make out, the drunk was bragging about the fact that he'd helped set up a meeting that would be attended by a bunch of big-time operators—that's the phrase he used, 'big-time operators'—during the last weekend in May. He figured he'd get a promotion out of the deal."

Abby clutched the sheet closer. "A promotion?"

"Within whatever organization he belonged to,"

Ryan explained. "At least that was my take on it at the time. But what really caught my attention was when he went on to mutter something about the cops being too stupid to catch on, that they'd never come sniffing around Demon's Acre. Which is a particularly barren area of the desert fairly close to the border," he added for Abby's benefit.

Her eyes narrowed in concentration. "And is that anywhere near where you crashed the next day?"

He had to smile, if only for a second. "You're right on target," he said, admiring how quick she'd been on the uptake. "To get back to the evening before, though, when I left the lounge and bumped into Mac, I was still trying to decide if I'd really overhead something important or whether it was just the quantities of liquor in the guy talking, given that the area around Demon's Acre hardly seemed a likely spot for any kind of big-shot meeting. By the time I got back to my apartment, I'd come to the conclusion that it was worth doing a flyby investigation if I got the chance."

"But you didn't say anything to anyone about it," Abby summed up.

"No. I wanted to check it out first." And that had been a wrong call on his part, Ryan admitted to himself. He should have said something, not just taken off on his own. Cocky. It could be argued that's exactly what he'd been. He'd certainly had little doubt back then that he could get to the bottom of the matter if there was anything of substance to what at that point could only be considered a rumor.

"Anyway," he continued, "my chance came the next day when I was out on a routine patrol mission, and I took it. For a while, I saw nothing more than most people familiar with the area would expect, which isn't much beyond desert vegetation covering a line of rolling hills separated by gullies. Then I noticed what seemed to be an entrance to an old mine shaft dug into the side of one of the tallest hills. I didn't think a whole lot of it until I dipped down for a closer look and got a glimpse of a shady-looking guard armed with an automatic rifle stationed near the opening of the shaft.''

Ryan snapped his fingers. ''And just like that everything clicked into place. To my way of thinking, there's only one sort of shady business that close to the border that would justify armed surveillance—the illegal drug trade.'' He met Abby's gaze. ''What looks like a mine entrance probably leads to some kind of underground operation. And if I'm right, it might be an excellent spot miles off the beaten path for a confidential meeting of 'big-time operators.'''

Abby's expression sobered. ''As in drug lords?''

''You got it. They could, in fact, be meeting there right this minute. It all fits, as far as I'm concerned. Trouble is, I have to convince the people in authority who can catch them in the act and give them one hell of a surprise.''

And convincing them wouldn't be easy, Ryan was forced to concede. When it came to his supervisors, he'd probably have to fight an uphill battle just to get them to believe his returning memory was sound enough to make what he was telling them credible. Then he'd have to lay the facts out in a way that would lead them to reach the same conclusions he had. And then he'd have to talk them into taking some fast action.

''Well, everything considered, you've convinced

me," Abby said. "This meeting could even support the theory that the fake Major Hobbs was keeping an eye on you."

Ryan mulled that over for a moment. "Makes sense," he allowed. "If the armed guard passed along the info that a government helicopter had been spotted in the area, and with the news that I'd crashed not too far from there the same day hardly a secret, I suppose the bad guys could have put two and two together and tried to cover all the bases by watching to see if I remembered anything that would put a spoke in their wheel before they took a chance on holding the meeting there."

"But after the major had to make an abrupt exit, do you think they'd still go ahead with their plans?"

Ryan shrugged. "I don't see why not. If this is a big operation, they probably wouldn't have stopped with the major. They'd have sent someone else to keep tabs on me, this time maybe from a distance. And if they did," he added, "all they've learned is that I've been going about my business in a normal fashion and was having a good time attending a dance last night."

"You're right," Abby soon agreed. "As things stand, they probably wouldn't view you as a threat."

"Too bad for them that I plan on doing my damnedest to be one," Ryan said.

Abby's brow furrowed in concern. "What will you do next?"

"Call Jordan Trask," Ryan replied after a second's consideration. "Before he left the Border Patrol to come here, he was highly thought of by the powers-that-be." *Higher than I was, that's for sure,* Ryan reflected ruefully. One of them—Jordan—had followed procedures to get the job accomplished. The other—him—hadn't always done things by the book.

Abby glanced out the window at a sky still more pink than blue. "You may wake him up if you call him now."

"I'll risk it," Ryan decided. "I have his number somewhere, but it'd probably be quicker to get it from Information."

"Okay." She retrieved a small notepad and pen from the nightstand drawer and handed them over. "I'm going to take a shower while you call." With that she rose and headed for her closet.

Ryan scooted over and picked up the phone resting on the nightstand. He watched Abby pull on her silky green robe while he punched in numbers. A part of him wanted nothing more than to lure her back to bed—and not to sleep. The rest of him, however, knew he had work to do.

Minutes later he was listening to the phone at the Trask residence ring. Ryan counted three and a half before it abruptly stopped.

"Hello," a deep and somewhat groggy voice muttered.

"It's Ryan," he said by way of greeting, recalling how during recent weeks he had stopped by for a few short and not altogether comfortable visits with the man on the other end. Now, for the first time since the accident, he could remember how much they'd enjoyed each other's company in the past.

Jordan immediately sounded more alert. "Anything wrong, flyboy?"

He had to grin. "You always called me that when you were beating me to a pulp at the pool table." He waited a beat. "And in case you forgot, I still owe you five bucks."

Dead silence reigned for a moment before Jordan let out a clearly relieved breath. "Jeez, am I glad to hear that."

Ryan nodded with satisfaction. "I'm back, friend...and I need your help."

HE WAS LEAVING. In fact, he had to leave as swiftly as possible. Abby understood the urgency of the situation. After spending hours on the phone in an attempt to convince the authorities just how urgent it was to take action, Ryan had won them over. Now he had to head south in the government plane being sent to pick him up at Harmony's small airport. That was the sole option at this point, since the only way he could pinpoint the exact location where he'd seen the armed guard was to go there himself.

Yes, he needed to go, Abby thought as she stood beside the front door holding a quiet Cara. Still, her heart was heavy with the knowledge that he'd be heading back to the life he'd led—and apparently had enjoyed leading—before the accident that had brought him to Aunt Abigail's. Later this afternoon he would be meeting with officials in Douglas, after which he would use a helicopter to try to retrace the path he'd taken on the day of the accident.

He would be flying again.

And all she could do, she knew, was wish him well and hope that he would not only be successful, but also come safely through what could turn out to be a risky situation.

Just then Ryan came down the center stairs, a nylon overnight bag Ethel had found for him in hand and his Stetson firmly settled on his head. He was dressed in his usual denim—jeans, shirt and waist-high jacket.

"I think I'm all set," he said as he approached with rapid steps.

Abby swallowed against the tightness in her throat. She'd already told herself that she would not make this a sober occasion. She had offered to take Ryan to the airport, but he'd opted to drive himself, so she would see him off here with a smile, no matter how much it cost her to produce one.

With that in mind, she put her lips to curving and had to hope her effort didn't appear to be as shaky as it felt. "Cara and I wish you luck," she said. Turning slightly, she opened the door on a perfect spring day.

Ryan stopped on the threshold and gazed down at woman and child. "I appreciate it." Leaning in, he reached out a hand and patted the baby's arm. "Thanks for the good wishes," he told Cara softly. "Now how about a goodbye grin?"

But Cara didn't grin, Abby noted with a downward glance. Instead, not even managing the smallest smile, she viewed the man standing before her with solemn dark eyes. *She's probably picking up on my worries,* Abby thought. One thing she had discovered in the role of mother was that babies could sense things even more acutely than adults.

"No grin for old Pips, huh?" Ryan asked wryly. He raised his gaze to meet Abby's. "Is she all right? I haven't seen her looking this glum since I got her out of the lagoon."

"She'll be fine," Abby replied as lightly as she could before her own smile slipped a notch. "Take care of yourself." She had to say it.

"I will." Ryan patted Cara's arm again, then

brought his lips to Abby's for a kiss that was nowhere near as hard and deep as many they'd shared, yet was somehow every bit as intimate. Straightening, he stared into her eyes for a long moment.

"I'll be back, crimson lady," he told her. And with that he was gone.

Abby watched him head down the sidewalk and turn to take quick steps toward the side parking lot. Then she closed the door behind him with a quiet click. She looked at Cara and did her best to summon another smile. "He *will* be back. We both heard him say so, and he meant it." But how long would he stay? That, she knew, was the real question.

Despite Abby's efforts to be cheerful, the baby didn't look any happier. She laid her head on Abby's shoulder and sighed.

"Tell you what," Abby said as she walked toward the rear of the house, "let's go out in the yard and play with your blocks."

Cara just sighed again.

The little girl perked up a bit once they were seated on a blanket spread over the grassy lawn. Her natural curiosity had her stacking and restacking her colorful alphabet blocks in different orders, and that whiled away the time until she issued a tiny yawn.

"I see a nap coming on," Abby said, and after pushing the blocks off to one side, she stretched out on the blanket with Cara held close. The sun peeked through fluffy clouds to sparkle down on them as the baby pointed and babbled at the birds in the trees. Then all was quiet as she slid into sleep.

Moments later Abby's ears picked up the first traces of what sounded like an airplane. The droning noise grew louder, until she shaded her eyes and stared up at the sky just as a small plane appeared. When it was directly over the bed and breakfast, the pilot dipped the left wing.

It was Ryan, Abby realized. He had always wagged a wing in just that way wherever there'd been a chance she was watching. Now she knew that he hadn't waited to reach his destination. He was in the pilot's seat right this minute learning firsthand how it felt to fly, and she could only guess at what he was thinking.

But she didn't have to guess about her own feelings. Suddenly how she felt was clear to her. Clear enough to have her eyes widening in response.

For all that she and the man soaring overhead had been divorced for years, for all that she had built a life of her own without him, in one respect—one vital respect—nothing had changed. At this very instant, and despite her recent resolve not to let herself care too much, Abby knew full well that down deep inside she had never stopped loving Ryan Larabee.

She not only cared. She loved.

HIGH IN THE SKY above Harmony, Ryan executed a deceptively effortless turn toward the border far to the south. A wide arc put them on the correct course as the plane responded with ease, as free as an eagle taking a path to the horizon on the strength of powerful wings.

"Man, you can really fly this puppy," said the light-haired man in his midtwenties seated beside Ryan in the narrow cockpit. "I swear it's humming under your hands. I've heard more than one rumor about how good you were, and it seems as though they were right on the money."

Ryan's mouth quirked up at the tips. "Thanks for the feedback. I'm glad the rumors panned out."

He was also glad that he'd accepted an offer to take over the controls. As he'd suspected, his piloting skills had quickly returned to their prior level, as if he'd flown just the day before, and the exhilaration sweeping through him, swift and sweet, felt as familiar as an old friend.

And yet something, he realized, was different. For the first time he could recall, he found the sheer thrill of mingling with the clouds battling with regrets at having to leave the ground behind. And not only the ground in the form of a small, friendly city rimmed by mountains. The woman who had seen him off on Aunt Abigail's doorstep with a none-too-steady smile was a big part of the package.

At least, though, he'd managed to win a smile from her. The baby in her arms had unfortunately been another story. There, he hadn't been successful, and that was one more reason for regret. It would have been good to see a tiny goodbye grin, even if the little devil had then gone on to get the better of him again by insisting he looked like somebody's granddaddy.

"I don't get to see this part of the state often," the man seated beside Ryan remarked. "My wife reminded me just this morning to put in for my vacation so we can take our two kids up north this summer."

"Sounds like a good idea," Ryan allowed as he skirted the mountain tops with their hefty load of tall pines. "You'll get away from the heat for a while, at any rate."

His companion chuckled. "And the blazing sun. My boys, the youngest being a toddler, are already even blonder than normal from running around in it all day long.''

''They'll probably enjoy it up north,'' Ryan said, making conversation as the miles slipped by.

''Yeah, they will. Then again, they usually enjoy wherever we take them. Kids are pretty adaptable, you know.''

''Actually, I don't know much about it,'' Ryan admitted. ''I'm hardly an expert when it comes to children.''

''Don't have any?''

''No.''

''Ever wish you did?''

Ryan frowned slightly. ''I may have to think about that one for a while,'' he said, considering the question. Had he ever somewhere along the way found himself wishing that he'd fathered a child?

No, but you had your chance once, something inside him replied.

Then in the blink of an eye he knew it was nothing less than the truth as other pieces of the past took shape to play out in his mind. Ryan stared straight ahead, dealing with the memories even as the skilled professional in him attended to the task of piloting the plane.

Yes, he'd had his chance, he couldn't deny, remembering now how Abby, a young and happy bride, had started to bring up the subject of a family after they'd been married for several months. At first, she hadn't pressed the issue when, caught up in his work, he'd sidestepped any real discussion. Then, as time passed, she'd become more and more dissatisfied with the long hours she was forced to spend without her husband—something he'd done his best to ignore or to make up to her in other ways—until finally one evening she'd confronted him with the fact that she wanted to have a baby.

"Not yet," he'd said, folding his arms over his chest and trying for an easy tone as they'd stood facing each other in the simply furnished living room of their small apartment. "There's no hurry. We have plenty of time."

"I have plenty of time for a child right now," she'd countered with calm determination.

"I don't," he'd told her.

Which was no more than pure fact. There hadn't been time for much else in his life back then. But, even more to the point, he'd had no inclination to assume a role that could well alter his life forever. Being a father meant accepting weighty responsibilities—responsibilities that would tie him down far more than those of a husband.

"Things are going fine as they are, with just the two of us," he'd contended, his voice hardening as his own determination grew to make her understand his position. "I don't want to change what we have. Not now."

And maybe not ever.

Although he'd never voiced those last words, they'd silently formed to hang in the tense air between them. And, understanding all too well, Abby had heard them—loud and clear enough to finally give up on their marriage.

That very evening, brushing aside tears, she had asked for a divorce with quiet dignity, packed her bags and left him still standing in the living room, where he'd raked his hands through his hair and cursed the fact that everything had fallen apart before his eyes.

But, even then, not for one minute had he contemplated changing his mind about having a child.

"God," Ryan muttered under his breath as the stark image of that evening faded. What had he thrown away that night? And what happened next, now that he had much of his memory back, including the piece Abby had deliberately kept to herself?

He released a gusty sigh. One thing for sure, he had a lot to consider before he saw her again.

Chapter Twelve

Abby gave Ethel a hand serving a buffet breakfast on Sunday morning to a houseful of guests eager to eat their fill before heading off for more of Harmony's weekend rodeo. Pancakes laced with warm maple syrup seemed to be the most popular choice for the hungry crew of visitors, although the silver chafing dish once heaped with fluffy scrambled eggs had received its share of the diners' notice and was now down to about half-full. As to the meats being offered, rounds of spicy beef sausage were currently winning out over lightly grilled ham slices.

"Can't wait to see more of those cowboys in action," one man remarked to his companions as Abby poured freshly squeezed orange juice into crystal glasses for the group around the table. "Calf roping yesterday was my favorite."

"I liked the barrel racing," said the woman seated at his side. "And those were cow*girls*."

"Today," another man said, "there's bareback-bronc riding, steer wrestling and bull riding. They usually save the bulls for last, maybe because they figure nothing else can top them."

The Western gear the middle-aged group wore confirmed the fact that they were a long way from veteran ranchers. Their bright and shiny outfits by no means resembled the softly faded garb Bill favored. Or for that matter, Ryan, who dressed the part to a T, even if he wasn't—

Abby broke off that reflection with a silent sigh. Somehow he had slipped back into her thoughts, despite the pact she'd made with herself after a sleepless night to put him out of her mind at least long enough to perform her hostess duties. It was, she recognized, a lost cause. With no word from Ryan since he'd left yesterday, she was too concerned to block out thoughts of him entirely.

Her practical side contended that he was tough enough to take care of himself in almost any situation. But almost wasn't good enough to ease her worries. She could only hope to heaven he was all right, and that she'd get some word soon.

Then she could turn her attention to other matters, such as how long she would have the man she loved in her life this time.

Not long, the voice of reason said.

And Abby could hardly argue the point. No one knew better than she did how tenuous their relationship had become now that Ryan had rediscovered how it felt to fly.

It would probably be wise to start steeling herself against an eventual parting. But that wasn't—couldn't be—foremost on her mind at the moment. Right now, his safety came first.

Abby made her way to the long oak sideboard and set down the half-empty pitcher of juice so the diners could help themselves to more. She was headed back to the kitchen when Ethel, again the image of a doting grandmother in one of her frilly aprons, walked through the doorway holding another stack of pancakes and a side dish of sausage.

"There's a call holding for you, dear," the older woman told her as their paths crossed. "A Mr. Dempsey."

Abby recognized the name as the colleague Ryan had bumped into on the evening before his accident. Leaving Ethel to deal with the guests, she made a beeline for the kitchen phone, trying to convince her suddenly pounding heart that it wasn't necessarily bad news because Ryan wasn't calling himself. Despite her efforts, it hammered against her ribs as she picked up the receiver.

"Hello, Abby Prentice speaking."

"Mac Dempsey," said a deep voice on the other end. "I'm calling from Douglas, Ms. Prentice."

"About Ryan?" Abby asked bluntly.

"That's right."

"Is he okay?"

"He's fine."

Abby's shoulders slumped in relief as she leaned one hip against the kitchen counter. He wasn't hurt—or worse. Thank God.

"In fact," Mac added, "he's a hero. Thanks to his info, the authorities conducted a raid last night and netted a bunch of guys drawing out plans for a new drug-smuggling network."

Now she could smile. "That's wonderful."

"Officials at the Border Patrol think so, trust me. They've been patting Larabee on the back for hours now.'' Mac paused. ''By the way, he asked me to tell you that one of the men caught red-handed was the major. He said you'd know what that meant.''

''I do.'' So they'd been right, she thought.

''Anyway, as I said, Larabee's involved with the government bigwigs at the moment, but he wanted me to let you know that he'd see you later this afternoon.''

Abby couldn't help but be grateful for that information. ''I'd appreciate it if you'd pass along the news that there will be a gourmet dinner waiting for him,'' she said, certain that Aunt Abigail's cook would insist on it. Ethel only knew that Ryan was on a hush-hush mission, but once she learned just how successful he'd been, she would want to celebrate in style.

''Actually,'' Mac told Abby, ''he said he'd like you to meet him at the rodeo going on in town.''

Startled by that statement, she stared down at the receiver. ''Why in the world would Ryan want me to meet him there?''

''I'm stumped on that one,'' Mac admitted.

''If I went,'' she said, ''he'd probably never find me in the crowd.''

''Hmm. I guess he must have figured you'd say something along those lines, because he said that you'd be able to find him. In fact, he drawled something about how easy it would be to locate him once he showed up.''

''That,'' Abby declared, ''makes no sense at all.'' Then she released a long breath. ''But I suppose I'll be there.''

''I'll let the man know,'' Mac told her.

"All right."

When the conversation ended, Abby hung up the phone and glanced over at Cara, who was seated in her playpen near the kitchen table. Today the baby was playing with her favorite toy horse, but not with her usual zest. She hadn't, Abby thought, been quite the same since Ryan left.

Attempting to provide some cheer, Abby walked over with quick steps and crouched down. "It's time to perk up in a big way, little dickens," she said, making her tone light, her smile wide. "You and I have a real adventure in store for us."

The baby looked up and cocked her small head at that announcement. "Ma?"

This time the familiar word so dear to her heart came out as a question, and Abby had to chuckle softly in response. "Yes, that's right, an adventure. The two of us are about to attend our very first rodeo."

ABBY WAS DETERMINED to hang on to her good mood when she arrived at the rodeo arena. After taking into consideration the sort of event she was—much to her surprise—attending, she was wearing the same ruby-red, Western-style shirt she'd worn to the dance, although she'd turned down the chance to try to squeeze herself into those jeans again. Her khaki cotton slacks would have to do, she'd decided.

Now a light, warm breeze swirled the air as she looked down at her companion, who was dressed in a bright pink top and pants, her dark curls held back by a matching pink headband trimmed in lace. Despite her cheery outfit, Cara still seemed quieter than normal as she gazed around with wide eyes.

"Well, it's pretty much as I thought it would be," Abby told the baby in her arms. "Crowded, noisy and...smelly," she summed up. "Then again, I don't suppose you can have a bunch of horses and cattle around without getting a whiff of them from time to time."

The outdoor arena itself was by no means new, Abby had noted when she'd parked in the dirt lot surrounding it. Located in the middle of a large, open area on the outskirts of Harmony, the round wooden structure was probably older than most of the city's residents. Nevertheless, Abby had to admit that it had a rustic charm all its own, maybe because it was filled with people of every age, plainly having a good time.

She went down a wide corridor toward the center of the arena, then turned to face the seating area and started to climb an aisle of steep steps. The lower seats were all taken, so she kept on climbing. Halfway up, she ran into the Stocktons, who were coming down.

"Well," Gail said over a particularly loud cheer from the crowd all around them, "fancy meeting you two here." She leaned in and gave Cara a quick kiss on the cheek. "These people make a lot of noise, don't they, sweetheart?"

"They certainly do," Abby replied when the baby remained silent. She noted that today her godmother looked exactly like a rancher's wife in a brown-and-white checked shirt paired with jeans and tan boots. "I wouldn't be here if it weren't for Ryan," she admitted, raising her voice to be heard. "He asked me to meet him here."

Gail smiled. "Ethel phoned to tell us the good news that he'd accomplished his mission and invited us for dinner tonight."

Yes, Ethel had wasted no time in getting a quick bulletin out, Abby thought wryly. Most of Aunt Abigail's guests had checked out that morning before heading to the rodeo, and now it seemed that a private celebration would be held there this evening. When she'd left the bed and breakfast with Cara, the cook had been knee-deep in planning a menu that was, some would contend, literally fit for a king. Or a hero.

A hero. Abby could only imagine how vindicated Ryan must be feeling right now. After everything he'd been through since his accident, she couldn't deny he deserved it.

"Bet Ryan will do justice to the food," Bill said with a twinkle in his eye. "Exercise usually makes a person hungry."

Abby frowned. "I suppose he would have gotten some exercise down south. The thing is, I'm still puzzled as to why he asked me to meet him here of all places."

The older couple exchanged a look. "We'd better be going," Gail said in the next breath.

Bill settled his wide-brimmed hat more firmly on his head. "Yep, I've got to get Lively ready."

"Lively," Abby repeated thoughtfully. "Isn't that the name of the huge bull you introduced me to when you gave me a tour of your place right after you got back from your honeymoon?"

"Uh-huh. He's going to show his stuff in the next

event,'' Bill explained, even as he started down the steps.

''We'll see you later,'' Gail added, following him.

And then they were gone, leaving Abby with her frown still firmly in place. Were those two acting a little strangely, or was it just her imagination?

Before Abby could give that question more thought, a soft voice coming from one side of her called out. ''Do you and the baby want to sit on the end of the bench here, honey? We can scoot over.''

Abby looked downward to find a fresh-faced blonde around her own age grinning up at her. ''No sense in your climbing any higher,'' the woman said.

''Thank you,'' Abby replied, and soon found herself seated at the end of a long row of rodeo fans suitably dressed for the occasion. She set the shoulder bag holding all the items travel with a baby required under the scarred wooden bench and settled Cara in her lap.

The blonde gave the little girl a playful wink, then looked at Abby. ''She's going to break more than a few hearts one day.''

''Yes, I suppose she will,'' Abby agreed with a small smile—one she imagined was visibly proud.

''With her coloring, she looks terrific in pink, just as you do in red,'' the blonde said with an admiring glance at Abby's shirt.

''I used to wear it a lot at one time,'' Abby acknowledged.

''But not anymore?''

''No.''

''Too bad. It suits you, honey.''

In a way it had suited her, Abby reflected. Not that

her mother, who considered *quiet good taste* three words to live by, had ever thought so. Then again, she wasn't her mother, and her new job no longer meant having to dress for success in the more conservative business world. If she so desired, she could wear every shade of the rainbow and let the colors clash all they wanted to with her hair. And maybe she would.

Another loud cheer went up just then, and for the first time Abby fixed her attention on the fenced-in ring below her. There, she saw a cowboy doing his best to bring a large and stubbornly uncooperative member of the cattle family to the ground with a desperate grip on the animal's twin curved horns.

"I suppose this is the steer-wrestling part of the program," Abby said, dropping a glance down at Cara, who was watching the action intently and still not making a sound.

"It is," the woman beside her replied, clearly having caught Abby's comment. "I take it you don't go to rodeos much."

Abby shook her head. "Actually, this is my first."

The blonde's lips curved in another grin as bright as the shiny snaps on the daffodil-yellow shirt she wore. "Well, you have a real treat in store for you. They're about to declare a winner in this event, and the bulls are up next."

"So I understand," Abby said a tad dryly, recalling how Bill had so hastily departed minutes earlier—almost as though a ton of beef on the hoof bent on total destruction was breathing down his neck.

"My hubby and I," the woman indicated the denim-clad man on her other side with a slight dip of her curly-haired head, "we wouldn't miss seeing the bulls for anything."

Abby's brows drew together. "Isn't it dangerous to ride them?"

"It can be," the blonde allowed, "but both animal and cowboy do put on quite a show."

Which Abby discovered for herself several minutes later as the first of the contestants, animal and rider, were introduced over the loudspeaker and a bull charged out of a narrow chute with a cowboy on his back. As it happened, the ride soon ended as the cowboy bit the dust, and the announcer said something about it being too short to count for a score. But that was only the beginning. Other contestants quickly followed and many earned points. Abby had no clue as to how they were tallied, but the higher the score, the more noise the crowd made.

As the event continued, her attention gradually drifted and she began wondering when Ryan would arrive. It was getting late, she saw with a glance at her wristwatch. But that was no reason to start worrying again, she assured herself. He'd said he would be here, so he would, eventually. All she had to do was locate him once he showed up...somehow.

"And the next bull up is Lively," the announcer said, winning Abby's full attention. "For those of you who don't know, he's a veteran on the circuit. Many of us haven't seen him in action, but we've heard tales about him. And riding him today is a newcomer to the Harmony Rodeo. So let's give a big hand to Lively and Ryan Larabee."

Abby's jaw dropped. Before she could even blink, never mind think, a huge bull she vaguely recalled seeing once before surged out of the chute. His rider, on the other hand, she recognized all too well. She forgot to so much as breathe as the aptly named Lively executed a high jump, did a fast spin and starting bucking while Ryan, by some miracle, managed to remain on top of a powerfully muscled back through it all.

"He's crazy," she murmured, finally regaining her breath. "He has to be."

"Who's crazy, honey?" the woman beside her asked, but Abby barely heard her, much less even considered replying. Instead, everything inside her braced tight with tension, she kept her gaze riveted on the ring.

Then Ryan went sailing through the air and she was on her feet as her temper flared at his deliberate disregard for his own safety. He'd barely landed in the dirt when she started down the steps with a careful grip on Cara, determined to give him a piece of her mind. Oh, yes. She intended to tell the man a thing or two, all right.

If, she thought grimly, he was still conscious enough to hear her.

IN THE RING far below, Ryan rose to his knees and sucked in a long breath, replacing the one that had been knocked out of him just instants earlier. The announcer was saying something, but the buzz in his ears blocked it out. At least his brain was functioning, although all it seemed capable of forming at the moment was a single question. Had he done it—had he actually hung in there for the required eight seconds?

And then he had his answer as he looked back over

his shoulder and found the usually haughty Lively reacting far differently on this occasion. This time Lively's broad head dipped down to offer a deep nod of what could only be approval, as if to say, *Okay, you did it, cowboy.*

The sight had him rising to his feet and offering his own nod, after which the bull departed the scene with a surprisingly graceful flick of his tail while the crowd's cheers rose to new heights—a tribute to Lively more than his rider, Ryan imagined, and that was fine with him. He had no reservations about the fact that he'd scored, not now, yet he also knew that some of the seasoned veterans who had gone before him were far better riders. They deserved the prize and the glory of winning. He was content, because he'd done what he'd set out to do.

Damn, but it felt good.

Ryan brushed off his jeans and walked toward the fence, one part of him predictably aching from his hard landing. This time, however, he hardly felt the pain. With a last, sweeping glance around the ring he saw Bill and Gail standing close to the cattle chute and giving him an enthusiastic thumbs-up sign. He returned the gesture, then broke into a jog in order to clear the way for the next rider.

Once he reached the old, slatted-wood fence, he quickly climbed over and landed on his booted feet lightly enough not to stir up too much dust. Then he faced the crowd and searched a sea of faces filling the arena, from close by to the upper reaches of the stands.

Where was Abby? He knew she was there some-where, had sensed it from the minute he'd started his wild ride. And it had, as Bill had predicted, given him the edge he'd needed.

Now he couldn't wait to see her.

As it turned out, his patience was hardly tested before she came around a bend in the fence, green eyes blazing even at a distance, and stalked her way over to him, her cheeks nearly flushed enough to match the color of her ruby shirt. Uh-oh, he thought. But he still had to smile at the sight of her and the wide-eyed baby she held.

"Ryan Larabee," she told him in no uncertain terms, "you have got to stop riding bulls!"

He had to wonder if she realized how wifely she sounded. Whether or not she did, though, her no-nonsense tone was music to his ears. And to his ego, as well, he had to concede. She did care about him, and now his chance was coming to demonstrate a few things to her, too.

He thumbed back his black Stetson and bided his time until she came to a halt a step away. Then he said, "I promise to stop riding bulls, if you promise to stop being my ex-wife."

That brought her up short and had her goggling for a moment as the noise of the crowd seemed to recede in the background. "There's only one way I can stop being your ex-wife," she got out, her voice softer.

"You are sharp, crimson lady," he told her with another smile. "The only solution, which I guess you and I have both figured out, is for you to marry me again."

As he'd half expected, much as he would have liked otherwise, she didn't rejoice at that news. Instead, her face settled into solemn lines as she studied him before finally speaking. "I can't go back to the way things were, Ryan."

His expression sobered to match hers. "Trust me, I don't want that, either." He hesitated, still seeking the right words after hours of considering what he would say. Once words had come easily to him, he recalled. Charming words that he'd seldom had to grope for. Now he figured his best bet was to opt for the truth.

"Flying is still important to me, Abby. I won't kid you about that. But it's no longer the most important thing in my life. You are." He paused for an instant. "I want—need—to make a life with you, one that includes a special little girl," he said with a look down at Cara, "and the babies we'll make together. I want us all to live as a family in the bed-and-breakfast gingerbread house, and I want it badly."

Abby was back to staring at him with what appeared to be sheer disbelief as he forged on. "I still have to make a living, of course, and after seeing the bogus Major Hobbs again—this time when he was hauled off in handcuffs—I got to thinking about something he once said that Ethel passed along."

Abby still looked dazed. "I guess I'm not following you."

"He suggested that Harmony might get more visitors if it had a weekend commuter service based at the local airport. The guy might be a crook, but I think it's a good enough idea to investigate starting up a small operation. In fact, I think it could be successful. But no matter if it's successful or not, I've got my priorities straight."

Ryan took in a breath, knowing his future might

well hinge on whether he could convince this woman that he truly meant what he was about to say. As far as he was concerned, he had no doubts. Since leaving Harmony yesterday, he had come to some firm conclusions by looking gut-deep inside himself.

He supposed a sensitive man might say he had looked into his soul.

"And those priorities," he continued with staunch determination, "are that our marriage comes first. Then our children, all of them, and the rest of our extended family, which I like to think would include Ethel, Gail and Bill. And then it's my job."

"Ryan—" Abby began.

"No, wait." The many doubts he could still make out in her gaze had him breaking in. Again he groped for words, realizing it wasn't only how he felt about flying that was the problem. "While I was away I remembered what I told you years ago about not wanting to be a father. I meant it then, I can't deny. As strange as it seems, I think I had to lose my memory and come to Harmony to recognize what I threw away that night. But, whatever the case, I know it now, and I'm dead certain that I want it back."

Abby filled her lungs with a steadying flow of crisp air, wondering if she could truly believe that. She wanted to, yes, but... "Are you really willing to change your whole life?"

"Yes," Ryan told her without hesitation.

"Even now that you can return to your job down south with full honors?"

"Yes." Again it was a short, firm statement.

But, again, she still couldn't quite believe. "Why?"

He reached out and brushed a rough-skinned finger over her cheek. "Because I love you."

Oh, how she'd needed to hear that, she thought as something inside her warmed at the words.

"And because," he added, "I'm not the same person who arrived on Aunt Abigail's doorstep weeks ago." Ryan raised his head and aimed a look around him, then returned his brilliant-blue gaze to Abby's.

"This place," he told her, softly and seriously, "really *has* made a new man out of me."

Believe him, her heart seemed to whisper, urging her on. And all at once she did.

"I love you, too," she said at last. "I always have. I always will. So I'm going to stop being your ex-wife." Leaning in, she stood on tiptoe to bring her lips to his. "And I think you'll make a wonderful husband...and father."

The kiss that followed was one of hope, of new beginnings, and although it lasted only seconds, it sealed the bargain between them, one Abby looked forward to sealing again, with even more enthusiasm, later than night. And the best thing about it was, she knew Ryan felt exactly the same way.

Just then, Cara clapped her tiny hands, winning the adults' attention. She hadn't spoken for hours, but now her eyes lit with a merry gleam as she stared up at the man standing inches away and issued one word that thoroughly summed up the situation.

"Da!"

Ryan froze for a moment in response. Only his throat worked as he swallowed hard to clear it. Then, moving in to close the last gap between them, he caught both woman and child in a wide embrace and gazed down at the pint-size girl who had just declared him a daddy.

"Well, little angel," he told her, his voice heavy with emotion, "you finally got it right."

Yes, *right* was the word, Abby thought, as happy tears suddenly welled up at the sight of the two most important people in her life viewing each other with growing grins while the crowd cheered another rider in the background. This time things were unquestionably better. And wonderfully different.

This time, she and the man she had loved for so long had it right at last.

*   *   *   *   *

Be sure to look for more books in
Sharon Swan's
WELCOME TO HARMONY
series coming soon from
Harlequin American Romance.

Say "I do" with

HARLEQUIN•

AMERICAN *Romance*®

and

Kara Lennox

How to Marry A HARDISON

**First you tempt him. Then you tame him...
all the way to the altar.**

PLAIN JANE'S PLAN
October 2002

Plain Jane Allison Crane knew her chance had finally
come to catch the eye of her lifelong crush, Jeff Hardison.
With a little help from a friend—and one great big
makeover—could Allison finally win her heart's desire?

Don't miss the other titles in this series:

VIXEN IN DISGUISE
August 2002

SASSY CINDERELLA
December 2002

HARLEQUIN®
Makes any time special ®

Visit us at www.eHarlequin.com

HARHTMAH2

$\mathcal{F}$ALL IN $\mathcal{L}$OVE
THIS WINTER
WITH
HARLEQUIN BOOKS!

In October 2002 look for these special volumes
led by *USA TODAY* bestselling authors,
and receive a MOULIN ROUGE VHS video*!
*Retail value of $14.99 U.S.

See inside books for details.

**This exciting promotion
is available at your
favorite retail outlet.**

Only from

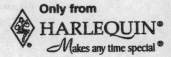

©2002 Twentieth Century Fox Home Entertainment, Inc. All rights
reserved. "Twentieth Century Fox", "Fox" and their associated logos
are the property of Twentieth Century Fox Film Corporation.

Visit Harlequin at www.eHarlequin.com   PHNCP02

Princes...Princesses...
London Castles...New York Mansions...
To live the life of a royal!

In 2002, Harlequin Books lets you escape to a world of royalty with these royally themed titles:

Temptation:
January 2002—*A Prince of a Guy* (#861)
February 2002—*A Noble Pursuit* (#865)

American Romance:
The Carradignes: American Royalty (Editorially linked series)
March 2002—*The Improperly Pregnant Princess* (#913)
April 2002—*The Unlawfully Wedded Princess* (#917)
May 2002—*The Simply Scandalous Princess* (#921)
November 2002—*The Inconveniently Engaged Prince* (#945)

Intrigue:
The Carradignes: A Royal Mystery (Editorially linked series)
June 2002—*The Duke's Covert Mission* (#666)

Chicago Confidential
September 2002—*Prince Under Cover* (#678)

The Crown Affair
October 2002—*Royal Target* (#682)
November 2002—*Royal Ransom* (#686)
December 2002—*Royal Pursuit* (#690)

Harlequin Romance:
June 2002—*His Majesty's Marriage* (#3703)
July 2002—*The Prince's Proposal* (#3709)

Harlequin Presents:
August 2002—*Society Weddings* (#2268)
September 2002—*The Prince's Pleasure* (#2274)

Duets:
September 2002—*Once Upon a Tiara/Henry Ever After* (#83)
October 2002—*Natalia's Story/Andrea's Story* (#85)

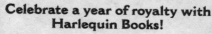

Celebrate a year of royalty with Harlequin Books!

Available at your favorite retail outlet.

HARLEQUIN®
Makes any time special ®
Visit us at www.eHarlequin.com

HSROY02

A
BETTY
NEELS
Christmas

What better way to celebrate the joyous
holiday season than with this special
anthology that celebrates the talent of
beloved author Betty Neels? Bringing to
readers two of Betty's trademark
tender romances, this volume will
make the perfect gift for
all romance readers.

Available in October 2002
wherever paperbacks are sold.

HARLEQUIN®
Makes any time special ®

Visit us at www.eHarlequin.com

PHBNC

COOPER'S CORNER

The latest continuity from Harlequin
Books continues in October 2002 with

STRANGERS WHEN WE MEET
by Marisa Carroll

Check-in: Radio talk-show host Emma Hart thought Twin
Oaks was supposed to be a friendly inn, but fellow guest
Blake Weston sure was grumpy!

Checkout: When both Emma and Blake find their fiancés
cheating on them, they find themselves turning to one
another for support—and comforting hugs quickly turn to
passionate embraces....

HARLEQUIN®
Makes any time special ®

Visit us at www.cooperscorner.com

CC-CNM3

buy books

♥ We have your favorite books from Harlequin, Silhouette, MIRA and Steeple Hill, plus bestselling authors in Other Romances. Discover savings, find new releases and fall in love with past classics all over again!

online reads

♥ Read daily and weekly chapters from Internet-exclusive serials, and decide what should happen next in great interactive stories!

magazine

♥ Learn how to spice up your love life, play fun games and quizzes, read about celebrities, travel, beauty and so much more.

authors

♥ Select from over 300 Harlequin author profiles and read interviews with your favorite bestselling authors!

community

♥ Share your passion for love, life and romance novels in our online message boards!

learn to write

♥ All the tips and tools you need to craft the perfect novel, including our special romance novel critique service.

membership

♥ FREE! Be the first to hear about all your favorite themes, authors and series and be part of exciting contests, exclusive promotions, special deals and online events.

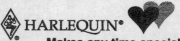

HARLEQUIN®

Makes any time special®—online...

Visit us at
www.eHarlequin.com

HINT7CH